Abe's Caribbean Takeout

Abe's Caribbean Takeout

Other Short Stories and Poetry

M. McLeary-Graham

To order additional copies of this book, contact:
Xlibris Corporation
1-888-795-4274
www.Xlibris.com
Orders@Xlibris.com
45504

CONTENTS

All my love to
Warren, Shari and Brianna
God Bless.
Peace and love to Mom, Yvonne, Shirley,
Joan, Clive, and the family fold.
Luv ya!

ABE'S CARIBBEAN TAKEOUT

In all my forty-two years I never thought that the smell of warm freshly baked bread would leave me feeling anxious, tired and fearful. The aroma filled the spaces inside the small bakery and Caribbean take-out my husband and I managed in North Miami-Dade. Giant glossy posters of Caribbean seascapes lined some of the walls; advertisements for international phone cards, Western Union, Air Jamaica and Appleton Rum. The shop faced a parking lot in a small strip mall on State Road 7 a few miles south of the Broward County line; within a stone's throw of a Jamaican record store, a Trinidadian fish market and a Bahamian hair salon. We captured a lot of hungry customers of all creeds, colors and languages. Business was good. It all felt good . . . until yesterday.

The smell and the warmth of the bakery reminded me of my husband Abe, the best bread maker from out of Spanish Town, Jamaica; the only man I knew who'd been in the pattie-shop and take-out restaurant business from he was knee-high to a mongoose, as Abe would say. He was a man who could seduce any taste-bud with his offerings of curried goat and ox-tails in the most mouth-watering sauces; festival and fried fish, sweet fruit buns, and the best patties in town. The smell of Abe's Caribbean Takeout normally hugged and caressed me lovingly the way my Abe would do when he was here.

But Abe wasn't here.

He had been taken in the night. *Taken in the night.* The thought spasmed inside my brain like a morbid headache.

Two men dressed in dark suits and ties, along with four uniformed Broward Sheriff's deputies, came upon the doorstep of our Miramar home last night, wielding shiny brass IDs and flash lights. They gave Abe two alternatives: Come peacefully or be taken in hand cuffs with guns drawn.

My screams of distress must have woken the neighbors who probably thought I'd called the police on my husband for domestic abuse. They couldn't have been more wrong.

One of the two dark-suited men spoke in a monotone that gave me goose bumps and sent a chill up my back.

"State your name, sir," he said.

"Abe Naranj."

"State your full name, sir," he said again.

"Abdul Narweed Naranj."

"We are taking you in for questioning."

"Am I being arrested?"

"No. We need you to help us with our investigation."

"What investigation?" I screeched.

"Please remain calm, Mrs. Naranj."

"If you are taking away my husband then you must be arresting him. What is the charge?"

"We will be holding him for questioning under the Homeland Security statutes," said one of the dark-suited men.

"Homeland Security!" My voice sounded alien to me. It quivered as my words came out in hysterical shrieks. "911. My husband is not a terrorist. What do you mean *homeland security*? Just what the hell do you mean?" I glared at the man's narrow nostrils and thick eyebrows, dark and bushy against his pallid skin.

Suddenly an oppressive heat swept over me, like a blast of moist hot breeze before a tropical downpour. I heard a sound in the shadowy hallway off from the living room and our two teenage children Sophia and Michael appeared, moving cautiously, hesitantly. Sophia, looking thin and waifish in an oversized T-shirt, spoke first.

"Mom, what's going on? W-why are they putting Daddy in handcuffs?" Her mouth began to tremble violently. So did the hands she held up in front of her lips. She started breathing strangely, sucking in gulps of air and not breathing out. I was convinced she was about to faint.

Although Michael said nothing, the look of terror on the boy's face broke my heart. For a fourteen year old boy to see his law abiding father being led away in handcuffs totally devastated him. Seeing my kids in the living room as a witness to this strange surreal moment unfolding like a nightmare forced me to control my own behavior and calm down for their sakes.

One of the uniformed officers took me aside and tried to assure me that this was "just routine" and nothing to worry about.

What was routine about this? Did they go around removing people from their homes at eleven o'clock every night and just happened to pick our house at random? I couldn't help but wonder if this had anything to do with Abe's immigration status. Were some of these people from the Immigration and Naturalization Service?

I asked the two men in the suits to repeat who they said they were.

"I am Lead Agent Tim Shatsky from the Federal Bureau of Investigations."

My face crumpled into one twisted scowl of confusion. "FBI?"

"And I am Agent Dan Scaroli also with the FBI."

The rest of that night got sucked into the spinning vortex of my confused memory. After they drove away with Abe, my children and I collapsed into one big weeping heap on the sofa. Agent Scaroli and a uniformed officer remained behind. I wanted to make some phone calls, first to Abe's mother, then to my mother. Then to an attorney friend that Abe knew. Agent Scaroli told me to hold off making any calls until he'd finished asking me some questions.

How long have you known Mr. Naranj? How long have you and he been married? Where was he born? Where were you born? Did you meet him here in South Florida or did you meet him in Jamaica . . . ?

My name is Diana Endine Naranj. I was born in Spanish Town, Jamaica. Abe was born in May Pen, Jamaica. We met at Spanish Town High School. My racial heritage is of African decent. Abe's racial heritage is of South Asian decent, Indian. None of his recent ancestors have ever visited India or Pakistan, just as how none of my recent ancestors have ever visited Africa (or if you count Scotland on my great-grandfather's side).

For their part, the police were tight lipped, unwilling to give me more information about why Abe was taken except to say that he was wanted for questioning in a case that had possible Homeland Security and Patriot Act breaches.

When they mentioned Homeland Security I remembered that before 911 there was no such thing as Homeland Security. After 911, I remembered hearing people talk about racial profiling. All over New York and New Jersey, they were picking up people who looked pretty much like my Abe.

We live in South Florida. The police could haul me in front of a judge right now and I can testify the truth of what I know about Abe.

Abe was a loving, humble man. He was humble from childhood. He grew up in abject, grinding poverty. On a visit to Jamaica early in our seventeen-year marriage he took me to the hillside where the shanty house he grew up in used to stand. That particular house wasn't there anymore, thanks to Hurricane Gilbert, but the surrounding environment still existed—dirt roads, flimsy zinc roof tops, no indoor running water. What saved him from total destitution was when his mother took him and his older sister to help out in a shop in

Spanish Town. It was a pattie shop. A tall, skinny, old, black-skinned man who looked frail but was a demon with an ultra-sharp machete sent the children to collect empty bottles from the street to bring back for the old man to trade in for reimbursements from bottling companies. Abe's mother worked at the shop and was finally able to send the children to school, but as Abe grew older, the old man came to rely upon him to run the shop. Abe learned to make patties and came up with the idea for his mother to cook food to sell. Before long, the shop became a thriving business.

Abe's mother migrated to America. Five years later she sponsored Abe. He studied at Miami Dade Community College and went to work for Bellsouth Telecommunications. When I came to America I was sponsored by my father who lived in New York. I studied at Hunter College and got a bachelors degree in business management. Abe and I would have almost certainly have lost touch after we left Jamaica had I not come to Florida for vacation and met up with him again purely by accident, and the rest, as they say, is history. We opened the shop in Miami where we used to live but bought our first home in Miramar across the county line in Broward.

Abe liked his reggae music and got down to his Soca music, a blend of calypso and reggae. He'd come out of his former shyness and could talk-it-up with any Mr. Barman with a glass of rum and a toothpick stuck between his teeth.

"One of these days I want to open another take-out store," Abe told me one time as we sat on a bench at the Haulover Beach Marina facing Biscayne Bay. We used to stroll out there some Sunday evenings when the kids were younger. Back then there used to be a really hot bar and restaurant out there called *Sundays on the Bay* that closed down when the owner went out of business with a dark cloud of the law over his head. The glossy Miami go-fast boats stopped coming around as frequently as they used to. Only the charter boat fishermen would occupy the moorings, displaying their nursery sharks and catfish.

"When I open another store—maybe it will be in Lauderhill." Abe stretched and leaned back on the wooden bench with his hands behind his head. Sniffing the sea breeze and looking toward the shuttered structure of the old Sundays, he said, "If I had money I would take over this place and turn into a jumping night spot for the tourists to sample my Jamaican fare in a fancy stylish place with ambiance, huh?" He looked at me and laughed, reminding me of the boy he used to be a long time ago.

"Opening it up for catered weddings," I said, joining the flow of his dream. A pelican stretched out its wings as it landed on the wooden jetty. Michael, then eight years old, screeched with fear and came running to his father who drew him onto the bench beside him and hugged him. Sophie, skinny and long bodied at age 11, twisted one of her two long shiny braids in her hand and laughed at her brother.

Twenty four hours passed since Abe was removed from his home in the night and he had still not returned. By now his distraught mother, my anxious mother, angry relatives and friends had gathered to await word from a civil rights attorney who'd been referred to us by Abe's attorney friend who only specialized in personal injury cases.

Even the media showed up at one point: a female reporter from a local TV news station. Luckily, the civil rights attorney, Mr. Tildon Marshall, instructed us to refer all media questions to his office although Abe's mother broke ranks and talked to another curious reporter, weeping as she desperately pleaded her son's innocence. "I don't even know what they holding him for," she wept, her face obscured from the camera. "America is the land of the free. What happen to my son freedom?"

Two days later Abe came home. Tildon Marshall drove him home at around noon. Abe called me at the shop and told me to put Myra in charge and come home.

Abe was a changed man. Quiet. Moody. His facial features seemed to droop with deep sadness and internal reflection. His shoulders drooped so much he almost looked like he had no shoulder bones.

By the time I arrived home, the attorney was getting ready to leave. He couldn't wait any longer but told me to call him if I had any questions. Believe me, I had plenty. I managed to ask one of them before he left.

"Mr. Marshall, what did they say my husband had done to hold him in custody?"

"Mrs. Naranj, they came up with a lot of suspicions, in fact there is a huge investigation underway, but most of the information is so tightly guarded that not even the Freedom of Information Act can help you get your foot in the door. The investigation involves the search for the suspected leader of an Al Qaeda cell based in South Florida. Abe's name got pulled into their data somehow and he got red-flagged as a potential conspirator."

I put my hand over my mouth and my knees began to shake. I went to sit down on the sofa beside Abe. He looked dejected and shabby, in need of a shave.

"Mrs. Naranj, I will be working on your husband's case *pro bono*—."

"What?"

"*For free*. What has happened to him is a travesty. Even though your husband has done nothing wrong, it will take a while to have the red-flag removed from his name in the data systems. Next time he travels, there is a likelihood he will be stopped at the airport."

My anger regrouped and I could not remain seated.

"So how in hell did Abe's name end up in their system?" I yelled, perspiration prickling my skin.

"Call me at the office, Mrs. Naranj. In fact, make an appointment to come and see me, both you and your husband. We'll beat this thing. However, I'm already late for my next appointment."

After the attorney left I thought Abe and I could talk, but he wanted to be left alone.

That evening, I kept the kids away from him after he bawled them out over dinner. It wasn't like him at all.

In bed that first night, he turned away from me with his shoulders hunched, tensed. I offered him a cup of something hot to drink but he said no. I let him sleep.

The second night however, after a work day in the store that seemed like long hard drudgery, after the kids had gone to bed, I poured a glass of rum and Hawaiian punch for him and for myself and said,

"Let we go out on the back porch. We need to talk. You can't just come back in the house like this and act like you and me are on two different sides of a wall. That can't happen here, Abe. I won't let it. Let we go and have a rum around the back."

As we sat on the dim porch at the back of the house I gazed out of the mesh screen opening of the back porch at the quiet shimmering lake, glistening with the lights from neighboring houses under a late evening sky. A light breeze ruffled the palm trees in the darkness overhead. Abe sat in the chair next to mine. A strong potent odor drifted up from him to my nostrils but it wasn't the usual smell of his perspiration after a hard day's work at the pattie shop. In fact since coming home from the pattie shop this evening Abe had showered. This was a different kind of odor, strange. I've heard people talk about the smell of fear and something deep down inside me told me that this was it.

Abe sat forward, his back taut, his elbows resting on his knees. He had shaved. The light coming from the living room highlighted the straight strands of grey hair above his ears. I took a sip of my rum punch from the cup in my left hand, and I touched him with my right hand, sliding my hand up and down the tight muscle of his back beneath the dull plaid shirt.

"What did they do to you in there, Abe?"

Abe said nothing. He began to rock back and forth with his elbows resting on his knees.

I waited without prompting him further.

I savored the sweetness of the punch inside the burning tincture of the rum and almost forgot my question to Abe when he suddenly decided to speak.

"How you gonna make people truly safe from terrorists if you keep arresting or killing the people who are not terrorist? How can racial profiling save us from another 9/11 . . . . Boy, it's a thing I will never understand."

Suddenly energized by his words I stood up.

"Abe, we should damn well make a lawsuit!"

When Abe looked up at me through the dim light of the back porch I never saw his face look more haggard and weary as it did now.

"And sue who? Uncle Sam? We'd be in our graves long before you'd see a damn penny! Anyway, it looks like there is more to this thing than I thought . . . ." Abe's voice trailed away, leaving me dangling in painful suspense.

"What is it, Abe? I can't understand how they could just pick on a man like you who is a hard working man, who don't do no harm to anybody."

"Well, from the way things come about, it look like I must have harmed somebody. You want to know how my name got into their data base, Diane? It wasn't by accident. The police said it was because of an anonymous tip why they started to investigate me. They were investigating me—and you—long before they came to the house that night."

"Lord Jesus! I can't believe this!" I quickly sat back down again, my knees starting to buckle under the anguish. "You mean to tell me, we went through all of this based on an anonymous call to the police about us? Someone hates us that much that they will have the police waste their time, waste tax payers' money to investigate and harass innocent people? Who was it? Did they tell you?"

"They ain't gon tell me. But I hope they turn the tide back on whoever it was who caused them to waste their time."

Somehow I felt too weary to speak another word for the moment. I just sat there beside Abe, gazing out at the dark shimmering lake. I remembered a Psalm my mother used to read out loud sometimes. Psalm 140, I think it was. "*. . . Let the heads of those who surround me be covered with the trouble their lips have caused . . . . let slanderers not be established in the land, may disaster hunt down men of violence . . .*"

Somehow it applied to the injustice that had unfolded itself in our lives right now.

Suddenly I was energized again, but this time by anger. I stood up and walked towards the edge of the porch, my nose almost touching the mesh.

"Why can't the police tell us who made false accusations against us? We are in our rights to know who our accusers are."

"Diane, come to me," Abe said. He reached out his hand and waited for me to come close to him. I moved towards him and hugged him where he sat. He rested his head against my belly and put his arms around my waist.

"Diane, don't worry anymore. The police said we are clean, we are OK. We are just a stone they turned over in their wretched war on terrorism. They didn't find anything under our stone when they turned it over so they put it back. They will keep turning over stones and looking under them until they find something. We're OK."

"So what about the red flag Attorney Marshall talked about? If we're going to have that hanging over us for the rest of our lives, then we're not OK. Every time we come and go from Jamaica or anywhere, are they going to stop us at the airport and harass us? I can't deal with that. I hope the liar who falsely accused us to the police gets his or her stone upturned."

Abe sighed, a long deep sigh that sounded like a last breath, as though he could never inhale again.

"This whole thing makes me not want to trust nobody any more," I said fretfully.

"Marshall should be able to help us clear up this computer glitch," Abe said.

"And how long can he do this for free?"

"Don't know. He say he passionate about these kind of cases. We can afford to pay him. When the freeness run out, we pay him."

"Well I hope he can find out who gave your name to the police."

"It might be someone we know," Abe said. He released me and I sat back down beside him. "Then again it might be someone who thinks I look too much like the terror suspects they see on the nightly news."

"For heaven's sake, can people be that shallow?"

"When people are afraid, or vindictive, or plain envious, they can be anything they want to be. They can be great pretenders to."

"But who? Man? Woman? Who? From now on everybody that walks into our shop calling themselves friend and smiling and what-have-you, I'm not going to look at them the same way anymore. You see these neighbors around here," I lifted my hand and pointed at the lights surrounding the lake, "I ain't gonna trust them no more neither . . ."

I was starting to feel drowsy but one glass of rum never made me feel drowsy that quickly before. Abe's revelations took the wind out of me.

These were troubled times. When the winds blew, they scattered widely the seeds of mistrust and fear. After the rain and the tears, the seeds began to germinate, growing into towering forests in a landscape full of fear and mistrust.

The smiling happy-go-lucky Abe that I knew before his encounter with the agents of mistrust had changed into a stilted haggard tree of remorse and perplexity.

If they can't trust me, can I trust them?

Abe and I turned in for the night. I held him while he slept because whenever I released him he would toss and turn fitfully, unable to sleep, but sleep came to him when he was in my arms.

We opened the store early on Friday morning, one of our busiest days. Lots of people stopped in for their curried goat and Cola Champagne combos, patties for the kids. Folks didn't cook on Fridays. We cooked for them.

Lorraine came over from the hair salon to buy her fried fish at lunch time; chatty-chatty as usual, hair unkempt despite being a hairdresser who took care of other people's hair. Bobby from the record store and some of his dreadnaught friends came over for a pint of cow-cod soup each. Later in the evening a tired looking working mother with her kids stopped by to pick up some ox-tail and rice. Life went on as usual.

Abe and I breathed deep sighs of relief that the nightmare was over until it became clear to us that the attorney and the media wanted to keep the nightmare going. They wanted us to keep on talking about it, to petition our local congressman, to keep it percolating in front of our eyes. We just wanted to forget what happened.

We gently extricated ourselves from Attorney Tildon Marshall and hoped that he and the roving media cameras would go and find another stone that had been turned over by a couple of agents on a dark night.

I smiled at the woman who'd come into the shop with her children. I'd seen her in the store before, like so many other regulars. People we thought we knew.

Even the white American man who came in from time to time, who wore the wrap-around dark glasses; talked about his fantastic Jamaica vacations, getting blasted in Negril, cool-runnings, ire-man, Bob Marley-man. Dig-it! No problem, man.

Faces. Voices. Talk. Who can you trust any more? Who really has your best interests at heart in this world today?

"Give me a curried goat for the road," he said to Abe, adjusting his wrap-around glasses but not removing them.

"Let me have two patties instead of one," said the woman with the kids. I served her and watched her and her children exit through the glass door.

Outside I saw what looked like a police patrol car parked up with two officers sitting inside, seemingly with no intention of getting out.

"No problem, man," laughed the man with the wrap-around glasses, and waved at us as he left the store. He made a left turn, heading south. Within moments of his departure from the store, the police patrol car powered up, reversed out of its parking space and also made a turn, heading south.

THE PASSION OF MISS RIGHT

Sunlight brightened the fresh green hills to the north and sparkled on the blue waters of Kingston Harbor to the south. Jayda McHenley tucked her smooth fine shoulder-length braids behind her ears with her red-painted finger-tips and closed her eyes as the *Air Jamaica* flight circled over Kingston, preparing to land at Norman Manley Airport. She whispered a silent prayer for a successful landing and opened her eyes again. Beside her, seated next to the window, was her six year old daughter Natasha who seemed perfectly calm and unperturbed at the prospect of landing. She drew inspiration from Natasha and stopped herself from digging her nails nervously into the armrest of her seat. If a little child could be so brave, why shouldn't she?

Together mother and daughter peered down at the sweltering city and watched it sweep away out of their view as the plane banked to the right and continued its descent over the harbor towards the airport located midway the Palisados Peninsular.

Jayda clutched her arm rest tightly. These days it seemed her nerves were a wreck all the time. Returning to Jamaica for a vacation was an antidote she hoped would help her to recover from the trials and tribulations of the past two and a half years since her husband Trevor's death. His had been a slow, harrowing death from leukemia. A man still in his prime, Trevor was destined never to see Natasha grow up. After his death Jayda had been left to run the real estate business alone until she decided to sell it off to a former business partner who used to be Trevor's good friend. She took her share of the money, put it in the bank and found a regular nine-to-five job at a law firm in Fort Lauderdale.

For the past two and a half years, her life was one big breathless struggle, and only Natasha gave her life some worthwhile focus.

"Mummy, my ears are popping," said Natasha, her thick pigtails dancing around her ears.

"We'll be out of here soon, baby," Jayda said and nestled her chin against Natasha's head. To mute the queasy anticipation in her stomach, Jayda thought about the last conversation she had with her Aunt Vina who was to pick her up from the airport. Aunt Vina laughed a lot and spoke with cryptic double-meaning that Jayda could not understand but could only guess meant a surprise was planned. Hopefully, it would be a pleasant surprise to take her mind off work and the dullness of the past few years.

In moments, the plane's landing gear connected sharply with the runway and it taxied smoothly towards the terminal buildings. Jayda heaved a deep sigh and looked out at the row of palm trees bordering the runway at the soft blue Caribbean sea gleaming in the Friday afternoon sun.

The hushed cabin suddenly filled with the clicking of seat belts unbuckling and the flight attendant announcing that passengers remain their seats.

Jayda was to be met at the airport by her Aunt Vina, her mother's sister. Jayda's parents lived in Fort Lauderdale, Florida. They were U.S. citizens but they had a home in the island, a beautiful house in the hills above Kingston which they planned to return home to after retirement. In the meantime, Aunt Vina took care of the place. On the phone call last night Aunt Vina assured Jayda that her room was ready and waiting for her and Natasha.

Jayda patiently made her way through customs and emerged into the intense heat outside the terminal building where folks young and old greeted loved-ones with jubilant shouts, and men and boys vied with the porters for the chance of a tip for carrying baggage.

Luckily, Jayda didn't have too many bags and her porter led her directly to the plump waiting arms of Aunt Vina.

Aunt Vina was a stocky woman with a rich bronze complexion and dark brown hair worn in an untidy French twist. Frosted coral lipstick glazed her thin lips and her plump high cheek-bones deepened the corners of her smile.

"Jayda, what a way how you thin! Girl!"

Aunt Vina hugged and kissed her and then bent down to give Natasha a cuddle. Behind her was a young man with smooth olive-toned skin and brown curly hair cut short on the top and slightly longer at the back. His hazel eyes showed some mixed heritage in his bloodline. He was slim and of average height, wearing stonewashed jeans and a navy blue cotton shirt that fluttered in the breeze at his waist. The top buttons at his neck were undone, showing an abundance of dark chest hairs. Aunt Vina introduced him as Victor. His smile displayed a row of perfect white teeth, and frequently he moistened his lower lip with his tongue.

During the drive from the airport, Vina asked about Temona and Philip, Jayda's mother and father, and how was Florida, and life after Trevor. Jayda answered as many questions as she could but was cautious with the amount of personal information she divulged. After all, she didn't know Victor, but there was one thing she did know, and that was the unnerving way Victor eyed her as he loaded up the car at the airport and the way he stole glances at her through the rear view mirror as she spoke with Aunt Vina who sat in the front passenger seat beside him.

"Victor rent the efficiency behind your parent's house," Vina said.

Jayda also learned during the drive that Victor was an accountant in a small firm in Constant Spring who took the day off to drive Miss Vina to the airport to pick up her niece whom he'd heard so much about and whom he was glad to meet. Jayda learned also that he was divorced with no children. Aunt Vina nudged him playfully and laughed,

"Don't get too interested in my niece you know," she chuckled. Silence then followed as they all stared out the windows at their surroundings. The Toyota moved at a steady speed along the road that curved left and right against the Wareika foothills, and left Kingston Harbor behind as they headed into Mountain View, a hot and sweltering built-up section of eastern Kingston.

They got held up by a snarl of Friday afternoon traffic but before long they were up in the refreshing green hills way up over the city, passing residences with high green hedges, manicured lawns and sweeping terraces.

The most prominent feature of Jayda's parent's house was the high sweeping gables that made the house look like a swan about to take flight. It was a beautiful, house commanding breath-taking views of both the mountainside and the Liguinea Plain where Kingston nestled under a clear sky. The perspective gradient was certainly an improvement on the totally flat landscape of South Florida where she had lived for the past fifteen years.

Victor smiled warmly at Jayda as he unloaded her bags and waited for Aunt Vina to unlock the wrought iron gate leading to marble steps ascending to the wood-paneled front door. Jayda pretended not to notice Victor's furtive glances but even when she wasn't looking she could feel his stare burning into her back.

"Take Jayda bags upstairs for me, please," Aunt Vina said and Victor obliged willingly, his muscles bulging as he hoisted the largest suitcase up the stairs. Jayda didn't go up right away but kicked off her shoes and stepped down into the luxurious sunken living room, carpeted with a deep beige shag-pile rug and expensively furnished with a mixture of Queen Ann and contemporary styled furniture her parents purchased in America and shipped down. On the far side wall glass portals opened out onto a tiled terrace overlooking the lush green lawn, the high wrought-iron fence and the trees and roof-tops of neighboring houses. The place looked better than she remembered it on her last trip home three years ago.

"Your Aunt Judette coming over later. Girl, she long to see you. She and Brandon came over from England last week," said Aunt Vina. "They'll be coming too." Brandon was Jayda's cousin. Auntie Judette was another one of Temona's sisters.

Victor appeared at the top of the stairs and began to descend, moving slowly so that his well defined thigh muscles rippled firmly beneath the material of his jeans. Although Jayda tried to ignore it, she could almost smell the sensual aura oozing from this man, his body language, the constant eye contact, the way he rubbed his upper chest with the palm of his hand, fingers outstretched. There was something persistently raw and sexual about him, detectable just below the surface of his soft spoken persona, and the signals he kept throwing her way did not flatter her but instead made her inclined to withdraw from him. It seemed that these days since the death of her husband she wasn't in the mood for man-hunting or hooking up with anyone right now. She just wanted to get on with her life, raise Natasha the best way she knew how, and not get into any situation that could lead to heartaches and heart breaks. If an interesting man should come along and the time was right, by no means would she stop the process. But right now she wasn't interested.

As Jayda and Vina lingered in the hallway an elderly man appeared in the kitchen, dark skin contrasting with white hair. He was dressed in brown pants and a white cotton shirt.

"Wilbert!" Jayda exclaimed and went to hug him. He was the gardener and caretaker, a man who'd been with the family for many years, even before Jayda was born. Wilbert kissed her and then stood back and admired her.

"You look like a goddess, Miss Jayda. America 'gree wid you!"

"And Jamaica 'gree wid you!" Jayda smiled and hugged him again.

The old man couldn't stop marveling at how much Natasha had grown. She was only three at the time of her last trip to Jamaica. "You' 'member Shaymus?" Wilbert asked Natasha.

"Yes, Uncle Willy! Where is he?"

"I'll show you in a minute," he said and after some more chit-chat Wilbert took Natasha by the hand and led her through the kitchen towards the back of the house to take her out to back yard and the family dog.

"The Burroughs might be coming by later, too. Or if not tomorrow. My goodness, everybody wants to see you. When are you taking Natasha to the country?"

"Monday," Jayda said. She planned to take Natasha to stay with Trevor's family in Clarendon and would probably spend the night there. That was the main purpose of the trip. Since Trevor died his mother hasn't seen her granddaughter. Jayda still wanted to make sure that Natasha stayed in touch with that side of her family.

"Are you leaving her up there and coming back?" asked Aunt Vina.

"Maybe. I'll let her spend a few days with them. If that's what she wants. Kids can be so funny. One minute Natasha begging to see Grannie and the next minute she doesn't want to see anyone but me!"

Jayda followed Aunt Vina into the kitchen where Vina reached into the fridge for a pitcher of lemonade and poured Jayda a slender refreshing glass. Through the kitchen window she could see Natasha petting the golden Collie. Beyond the back yard with its rose bushes and sprawling red hibiscus shrub along the back fence, the mountainside sloped majestically skyward. It felt wonderful to be in the mountains again, far from torrid flat lands.

Victor suddenly appeared again. He had walked around the outside of the house and was now by the back porch with Wilbert. Seeing Aunt Vina at the window he excused himself from Wilbert's company and came up to the back door.

"See the car keys here, Miss Vina."

"Thanks, Victor. You're a great help."

"Anytime, Miss Vina." He had a deep rolling baritone voice. Then he looked at Jayda and smiled. "Nice to meet you, Jayda. I might see you later."

He walked away down the tiled back porch to a door which led to the efficiency he rented. As he opened the door they could hear the voice of Bob Marley singing *"Could You Be Loved"* coming from the room.

"The man like you to death, but he better not like you too much!" Vina chuckled and folded her arms under her ample bosoms.

"What makes you think he likes me"? Jayda asked, shaking her head.

"You mean a grown woman like you can't tell?"

"I guess I'm just not interested."

"You're not flattered either?"

"No."

"Good," said Aunt Vina, pouting her fine lips. At that moment the telephone rang. Vina picked up the extension on the wall above the kitchen counter.

"Hello? Celia? She's here, yes! Here she is."

Celia was Jayda's best friend, a girl she knew and grew up with from elementary school. She was like the sister Jayda never had.

"Girl, I long to see you. I coming over this evening, OK, honey-bun!" Celia squealed.

Jayda was glad to hear her voice even though they had only spoken last week when Celia promised to show Jayda a good time when she got here.

When Jayda hung up the phone she decided she'd better prepare herself and Natasha for the evening ahead.

Up in the bedroom, the suitcases brought up by Victor were standing between the dresser and one of the single beds. In the middle of the dresser was a large ornate vase of flowers which gave the room a tropical splash of color. This was the very room Jayda had spent her childhood in and now here she was sharing it with her own young daughter.

She gave Natasha a bath and dressed her in a fresh clean cotton two piece short-set. She smoothed some hair-oil into Natasha's hairline that had begun to frizz slightly and brushed it before sending her off downstairs to watch TV while Jayda showered.

Jayda emerged from her shower moments later, dripping in herbal scented aromatic fragrances, her braids secured in a peach colored towel.

"You don't see the flowers?" Vina asked.

"Who could miss them! They're gorgeous!" Jayda exclaimed. "Thank you, Aunt Vina.

"They are not from me. You didn't read the card?"

Jayda looked puzzled. She glanced at the flowers then back at her aunt. "You didn't buy these flowers for me?"

"No. Go look at the card."

Bare feet sinking into the soft pile carpet underfoot, Jayda walked towards the flowers and searched for the card hidden in the spray of stems. She took the card between her fingers and read the greeting.

> *"Welcome home, sweetheart.*
> *All my love, Ray F."*

Jayda shook her head in disbelief, and her heart skipped a beat.

*

Ray F. Raymond Fennerman.

Seeing his name on the card in the flowers set off a train of thoughts and emotions that steamed like a locomotive inside her. For the rest of the day into the evening she kept thinking about Ray Fennerman.

He had been her first love. Celia, knowing all of Jayda's secrets, would call him "her only love".

Jayda had been in love with him a long time ago. A love so deep and so passionate, she was totally convinced that they were born for each other. Then one day it was as though he had pushed her soul headlong over a cliff and she found herself falling, falling painfully out of love, when he told her that he believed they weren't right for each other, that he wasn't ready for a commitment. Acting upon his "thought" he ended the relationship.

Jayda was devastated.

"Let's just be friends," Ray offered. "I'm not ready for commitment yet. Plus I don't think you're the girl I'm looking for . . . Don't get me wrong. It's just that—I don't know, it's just that . . . You're a nice girl and everything but I need someone who understands me more, who is more of a match for me and my goals. Somehow, I don't think you and I have the same goals and we'd probably make each other miserable . . ."

His voice seemed to echo so loudly through the years to this present moment, this idyllic moment as the sun set splendorously over the Liguinea Plain and the terrace above the pool deck clattered with staccato voices above the cool rhythms of instrumental reggae music . . . A saxophone playing "*Little Cottage In Negril*" and Dennis Brown singing "*Love Has Found It's Way* . . ."

It seemed like only yesterday that Ray uttered those heartbreaking words and offered as a replacement mere friendship. If she hadn't invested her entire heart, soul and body into the relationship it probably would have been easier to go along with the offer. It was more of a demand than an offer, a most humiliating demand. How could she simply reduce her intensely invested feelings to just friendship. He thought she wasn't right for him and he simply walked away.

Now here he was sending her flowers. Maybe she shouldn't read too much into the gesture. God, it was only a bunch of flowers. Anybody could send somebody a bunch of flowers. So what! She secretly urged herself to be cautious about jumping to conclusions. He was after all a nice guy who did that kind of thing for his friends.

Jayda and Ray had met while studying at University College in Mona. She was going after a degree in business management and so was he but he was already in his third year and pursued additional work that would take him further into undergraduate pre-law studies doing research in civil law. He had big dreams for his future. She wasn't to be a part of his dreams. Life became very awkward after the breakup, particularly as both she and Ray moved in the same circle of friends, a circle which included the man who would be her future husband Trevor. Trevor was studying social economics and accounting and he participated in the same social outings and debating societies and extra-curricular activities as Ray and Celia and others in their group. Ray graduated ahead of her and left his alma Mata to travel and continue his studies abroad. It was at this time that Jayda and Trevor began seeing each other but simply as platonic friends and study partners. Trevor emigrated to America before she did and it was fortuitous that they met up again after she emigrated to Miami with her family. At that time Trevor worked with a mortgage company in downtown Miami while studying at Florida International University. They each became U.S. residents through their parents' sponsorship. Before long a deeper relationship began to blossom.

Jayda and Trevor had a lot in common, but with Trevor it hadn't been love at first sight as it had been with Ray. With Trevor she started falling in love when she realized he wanted her in his life not simply to fit in with a goal he had mapped out in his own life but because he really wanted and needed her, and because he had much love of his own to give.

There was always a microcosm of guilt laying way in the back of her subconscious mind at the fact that she never felt that tremendous rush, the lustful fervor for Trevor as she had felt for Ray. She felt she should have been able to give Trevor some of that sensual heat but their's was an eternal love wherein the flame burned calmly everlastingly, not like some wild-fire burning hotly and rapidly hastening towards a speedy dousing of the flames, like the wild-fire she felt with Ray.

She considered herself privileged to have been the holder of the eternal flame even though during some of the rocky moments of her marriage she secretly yearned for the all consuming wild-fire.

Since her husband's death she wasn't interested in any kind of flame at all, not even an old flame. She'd been through enough fire, two miscarriages before Natasha came along; and witnessing the slow death of her husband. Her life had plateau'd out to a plain of nothingness and somehow she wanted it to stay that way. There was safety on that plateau of nothingness.

"You're looking lovely tonight," said a voice close to her ear.

Jayda gasped, the voice jolting her from her reverie. It was Victor, smelling of Old Spice and wearing tight beige pants. He had helped himself to some rum punch and came to sit down beside her on the terrace.

"Thank you for the compliment," she replied awkwardly. She could feel his eyes on her again, studying her from head to toe.

At that moment a car pulled in through the wrought iron gates and drove up the sloping driveway but because of several cars already parked there the car could move no further. The headlamps dimmed and out jumped Celia and her two children chattering loudly and laughing. From the drive they waved at those sitting on the terrace.

Jayda waved wildly, glad to see her best friend Celia and relieved to be able to get away from Victor.

Celia Kahn was a beautiful woman in her early thirties of a heritage mixed with Black and Lebanese. She wore her wavy brown hair in a blunt cut bob around her cheeks and her brown-grey eyes stared out from under well-shaped brows. However the quality of her skin was poor because of a previous condition of acne when she was younger.

She threw her arms around Jayda in a big hug and they strolled arm-in-arm into the kitchen, chatting animatedly, with Celia looking around in an exaggerated manner.

"Why are you looking around like that?" Jayda asked.

"He's not here," Celia sounded surprised.

"Who's not here?"

"Raymond Fennerman."

"Raymond Fennerman! You expected him to be here!" Jayda was surprised. She unlinked her arm from Celia's.

"Yes!"

At that point Aunt Vina showed up behind them as she entered the dining room from the terrace.

"My dear child, he's not here. Never came. Just brought flowers." Vina eyed Celia

"The night's still young." Celia sing-songed to Vina.

Jayda shook her head in bewilderment. "Celia, if you weren't my best friend, I'd tell you to mind your own business. I don't want you to do any match-making for me, especially not with some old flame. Definitely not with Raymond Fennerman." Celia ought to remember what Jayda had been through with him. Jayda didn't need to spell it out for the whole crowd to hear, and especially not with her aunt standing there listening.

"Look, Jayda," Celia threaded her arm through Jayda's and led her away into a quieter corner of the dining room. "Everyone makes mistakes. I've never seen a guy so intensely in love."

"With his own shadow," Jayda interjected.

"With you, Jayda, girl, with you."

"So you're his confidante now, are you?"

"Not so much a confidante as an old mutual pal who knows you all."

"A go-between then!"

Celia laughed. "Jayda, honey, listen to me. I don't need to do anything. Fennerman is man enough to make the moves on you. He doesn't need a go-between."

Jayda shook her head, half amused, half annoyed. "So he thinks he's bad and bold, eh? What happened? He never got married? He doesn't have a girlfriend? Let him use up his boldness somewhere else!" As Jayda spoke she shuddered as a memory flashed across her mind. A memory of a moment when Ray held her in his arms on the terrace of his parents' house high up in Stoney Hill during a pool party. The setting sun slit the belly of the sky with a streak of burnished gold. In a private moment intense with sensual longing and animal heat, Ray stole a kiss. He took her hand and began to lead her away from the noise and activities.

"Baby, come upstairs," he whispered in her ear.

"No, Ray," she whispered back. "This is your mother and father house and it is wrong . . ."

"Does it feel wrong to you?" he asked. They were now in the deserted utility room near the back of the house. He pulled her close to him and ran the tip of his tongue along the edge of her earlobe, sending electrical impulses through her which caused her knees to weaken and desire to pulse hard through her veins.

"It is wrong, Ray. We can't do this—"

He cupped her face in his hands and covered her lips with his, to silence her and to help dispel her trepidation. He knew that she had never been with a man before, little Miss Puritan with a streak of white-hot passionate potential. Even as grown-up college freshmen poised at the cusp of a brave new world she still wanted to hold back and not give in to her womanly desires, still girlish, still innocent and idealistic. But the moment was yet to come: the moment he would take that innocence in one swirling orgasmic moment of sheer bliss . . .

Jayda's mind came back to the present. She found herself breathing hard as though she had been submerged under water. Celia probably took her heavy breathing for an imminent tantrum, but when Jayda spoke she spoke calmly.

"He probably still thinks he's bad and bold. He was that for sure. But he blew it, Celia. He blew it. Afraid of commitment. Waiting for the elusive Miss Right. Whatever happened? Why didn't Miss Right materialize for him? It just went to show how much of a dream world he'd been living in. And still probably is living in since he is still not married."

"Don't judge the man like that, Jayda," said Celia.

Why not judge him? Jayda thought. Trevor was different. He accepted Jayda for everything she was. Together they went through the highs and the lows. They grew together. Trevor was mature enough to realize that no-one was born to be Mr. Right or Miss Right. People became Mr. or Miss Right after passing through the fire, plenty of emotional growth, stress and strain, coping. If a man was afraid of stress and strain, and coping with life's problems, then he would never find his true Miss Right. Miss Right didn't just fall out of the sky. Miss Right was a product of purging by emotional fire.

Ray Fennerman. A man from her past. Badness, boldness and kisses from so long ago.

The past was dead as far as she was concerned.

"I really don't want to hear anymore about him, if you must know."

"Like I said, people make mistakes."

"And he's using you as his spokesperson, Celia! Wow!"

"And people change too."

"Yeh, like a John Crow changing into a dove."

"Why are you so angry, honey-bun?" Celia's smile disappeared and she stared directly at Jayda.

"I'm not angry, Celia. Now let's drop the subject."

Silently they walked over to the large bowl containing the rum punch; lemon rinds floating on the red surface.

"Let's drink and get merry!" Celia suggested.

Jayda silently picked up a plastic cup and allowed Celia to fill it using a ladle that matched the crystal punch bowl.

"Where's Paul?" Jayda asked about Celia's husband.

"He's still in the States. He's due back next month." Her husband was a Jamaican with U.S. residency, just like Celia and Jayda. He traveled back and forth constantly for his banking business. He made a lot of money but he was hardly ever home.

Somebody turned up the music and some of the people on the terrace began to dance.

Celia encouraged Jayda to get down to some soca, as Vina and Judette and some of the female cousins began to wave their hips from side to side in time with the music, bending their knees and getting down as low as they could to hoots of laughter and cat-calls.

Afterwards, Jayda and Celia cooled out against the white painted balustrade around the wide tiled terrace. A cool breeze traversed the dark mountainside with its twinkling lights and embraced them. Celia lit a cigarette and blew her smoke away from Jayda.

"We're going to party like there's no tomorrow—before you go back to the States, girl. I have some friends we can go out with. I have a friend who has a club in Mandeville. Remember Chinnee? The guy whose father owns the big store in the plaza down the hill? He used to go to Excelsior High."

"Yes."

"That one. I going to make some plans."

"But remember I have to take Natasha over to Clarendon to stay with Trevor's folks. They haven't seen her since Trevor died and that's the real purpose of this trip."

"When are you taking her?"

"Monday."

"When are you going back to the States?"

"In two weeks."

"You have plenty of time."

Suddenly Victor approached them. The whiff of his Old Spice was tempered by the odor of cigarette smoke.

"What's happening ladies?" he said softly. Several more of the buttons of his shirt was opened revealing even more chest hair.

Celia looked him up and down. "Hi, Victor, how are you?"

"All right, you know," he answered casually, flicking away his cigarette ash.

Behind them the women were getting down to Arrow's *"Hot Hot Hot"*.

"You know Club Mystique?" he asked Celia.

"Yes, somewhere up in New Kingston," she replied, blowing out cigarette smoke.

"I want to take Jayda there," he said and turned his white smile upon Jayda.

"I don't know . . . When?" Jayda asked.

"Tomorrow night."

"She'll go if I can go too," Celia smiled. "Let us dance, you hear, child," she tugged at Jayda's wrist. "When this song plays I can never stop my hips from moving. Believe me, it is totally subconscious!"

*

The following night at Club Mystique Victor tried to keep Jayda on the dance floor for as long as possible but she soon tired and insisted on returning to the table. Celia was smoking a cigarette and talking animatedly with a young man who had recognized Victor and came to join them. The live band on the stage blasted into full swing, the reggae baseline vibrating the walls. Some folks on the dance floor applauded and cheered. During this time, Victor tried to get a little closer to Jayda. They talked, he about his job as an accountant at an insurance firm. She wasn't as talkative or forthcoming but he asked her about Miami and told her of his desire to one day live in the States.

The band played for forty-five minutes after which time they took another break. Victor excused himself to the restroom.

At that moment the DJ started playing discs again. The opening strains of Boyz II Men's *"Down on Bended Knees"* tumbled smoothly out of the speakers and Jayda took a sip of her rum and coke. She sat back to luxuriate as she listened to the song. Just at that moment someone touched her hands. A voice above her said,

"May I have this dance?"

She looked up to her left and found herself staring into the strong handsome face of Ray Fennerman.

Firm, well defined lips, dark skin as smooth and sexy as a satin sheet. Even though his face was more manly than it was over fifteen years ago, he still had dimples in his cheeks when he smiled. And here he was, smiling at her as he took her hand in his. Jayda realized she must have looked silly sitting there with her mouth hanging open in disbelief.

She wanted to refuse to dance with him but she felt herself moving sideways out of her seat and standing up, the top of her head stopping where his shoulders began. For the first time in fifteen years she was standing only a breath away from him. At one time in the past, they were even closer than a breath. Suddenly a memory came back to her in the pleasant whiff of his cologne, in the warmth of his smile, a memory of a moment when he encircled her in his strong, powerful arms and rested his chin gently on the top of her head. She felt warm and secure like a baby. She was his baby back then. Warm and secure at the core, flaming passion burning through her and reaching out to scorch him.

Their romance back then was set against college life, studying, getting away together at weekends to a North Coast beach, making love to the sound of ocean waves, Teddy Pendergast and Luther Vandross; the soaring highs and the pitiful lows, the lowest low coming when Ray decided to end the relationship.

Now here he was holding her in his arms again on the dance floor many light years later as though it were yesterday, as though a whole lifetime had not already gone by, changing her, changing him. Had he changed?

Jayda suddenly felt awkward dancing with him. She strained her body away from his, stiffening herself in his embrace. She wouldn't allow herself to relax in his arms, counting the moments until the song ended. Under different circumstances the ballad now playing would have been one she could have slow danced to all night. Instead, as memories of the hurt and loneliness swept back to her like the tide, she couldn't wait for him to release her so that she could return to her seat but he wouldn't let her go. The next tune to play was an old romantic number they used to daydream to, *"One In A Million You"* they used to slow dance to as though they were making love with their clothes on. That was how hot they used to be with one another but this was too much. She shoved him with insistence, letting him know she really didn't want to dance with him anymore.

He released her and as the song played they walked back to the table.

"I don't want to dance anymore," she said.

"That's all right. We can talk," he said as he led her by the elbow back to her seat. She tried to ignore that powerful, physical pull he seemed to have whenever he was near her but it was difficult.

When they returned to the table Victor was sitting there with Celia and Victor's friend Desmond. Victor made a big show of making room for Jayda and making sure there was no room for Raymond to join them.

"Hi, Raymond!" Celia called across the table. "Long time no see. What are you doing here?"

"Just stopped by to see what the action was like, and I like what I'm seeing," he said looking directly at Jayda. His eyes lingered on her, taking in her soft oval face framed by smooth glossy braids that curled under at her shoulders, and the smooth contours of her neckline. She could feel every inch of her skin tingle as his eyes swept over her.

At that moment Victor did something completely out of the blue. He reached over and pulled Jayda's face toward his and kissed her cheek. Then with a big smile on his lips he said,

"Having you here, Jayda, has made my night."

Jayda was too dismayed to respond. Her face began to tingle but this time with embarrassment. Jayda quickly pushed him away, mouthing the words, "What are you doing!" but no sound came out. She was so embarrassed she couldn't look at anyone except Celia who looked equally surprised. Ever since Ray showed up at the club Jayda had guessed that his presence had something to do with Celia. It was more than likely that Celia had tipped him off that they would be at the club.

Jayda's stare turned cold as she tried to send messages to Celia with her eyes. Celia quickly regained her composure and inquired,

"Victor, is why you do that, man? Don't you see you are embarrassing the lady."

He laughed a strange little laugh and sipped his rum and coke.

When Jayda chanced a look at Raymond his demeanor had changed. He suddenly seemed impatient as though he had somewhere else more pressing to go to.

Jayda asked to be excused to go to the restroom. As she passed Raymond he touched her arm and said briefly,

"We'll talk, you hear."

Jayda took one last look at his face, realizing that by the time she returned from the restroom he would most likely be gone.

Celia followed her.

"You arranged for Raymond to be here, didn't you?" Jayda said angrily.

"Yes, I did. Why are you so angry?" Celia's light brown eyes glared at her.

"B-because—because look what has happened!"

"I didn't know what was going to happen, Jayda. But I suppose you do care what Raymond thinks," Celia's mouth curved slowly into a smile. "Miss. Jayda, I just don't get you at all. Don't be angry with me. Be angry with yourself. You're the one who's all confused."

Jayda didn't know what to say. She watched Celia walk out of the ladies' room, leaving her there to contemplate her next move.

*

Jayda spent Sunday at Celia's house. The children played Nintendo in the play room and Jayda and Celia relaxed by the pool. Every so often Celia would go in and check how dinner was progressing. Her housekeeper Mrs. Jaspers was reputed to be a first class cook.

Celia brought out long glasses of Hawaiian punch laced with rum, and they lounged in sun chairs in the shade of umbrellas.

"I'm mad with Victor," Celia said.

"And I'm mad at you," said Jayda.

"That's not fair, Jay. You can't be mad at me. I knew you were glad to see Raymond again. Weren't you? Be honest and admit it to yourself! Girl, that's one fine piece of man there."

"How come you never tried to snap him up, Celia?" Jayda asked.

"Don't you think I've tried to give that man the eye a few times? He's good friends with Paul. Raymond might be a guy that loves women but he's a man of principle. He's not going to mess with a married woman, and least of all with his friend's wife! I tell you, if I were a single woman like you, I'd be in there with a chance!"

Jayda grinned. Celia had no scruples at all when it came to flirting around. She was married but it didn't matter in the slightest that she would act upon her desires for another man, if the other man gave her an opportunity for an affair.

Celia got up and went into the living room to turn on the stereo and find a tape to play.

The soft warmth of the sun embraced Jayda's body as she lay in the shade of the huge striped umbrella beside the sparkling pool on a vast terrace high above the city. Celia's house was higher up the mountain from where Jayda's parents' house was located. Up there, Jayda was closer to the sky, closer to the breath of God. She could stare at the soft white belly of a lazy cloud rolling southwards into the blue yonder and feel free.

Her sunglasses softened the glare from the sky and from the splintering gleam of the sunlight on the swimming pool. She took a deep breath of fresh mountain air and examined her freshly painted nails before closing her eyes again, stretching one arm above her head on the pool side recliner chair. Then came the opening strains of Roberta Flack's gentle vocals singing *The First Time Ever I Saw Your Face . . .*" drifting across the pool deck, across the marble terrace from the open glass doors of Celia's living room. Suddenly a burning sensation filled Jayda's head as though she had just inhaled water. It was a dizzying sensation, the kind that besieged someone when they were overtaken by a distant memory that came charging at them like a runaway train.

Her relationship with Raymond had been like a runaway train that flipped off the tracks, a train wreck she thought unsalvageable. Jayda and Raymond made love for the very first time in a room at the top of his parents' house, on a Wednesday afternoon when the entire place was deserted except for the family dog. Jayda had just turned nineteen and Raymond was four years older. He picked her up from U.C. and he ignored her protests that she needed to take her books home and study and do a million and one other things. He even ignored her protests against "violating" his parents' home by doing something like this in their house. He had laughed at her use of the word "violating".

"You think I'm going to violate you too?" he chuckled, embracing her in the deserted tiled hallway that led out to the kitchen. Close by were the steps leading upstairs.

"No, you won't be violating me, Ray. You'd be making love to me."

"Don't you want that, Jayda?" he breathed close to her ear.

"Of course I do but—"

"Then come upstairs with me, baby. My parents won't be back for hours. Please. I'll take good care of you . . ."

And she followed him upstairs. In his room behind locked doors as the bright hazy afternoon sunlight slanted in through his half closed blinds they made love on his double bed to the sound of sexy soul music coming out of his bedside boom-box. Roberta Flack was in there somewhere . . . which was why her vocals suddenly brought the memories flooding back to Jayda as she lounged beside Celia's pool. Tears burned Jayda's eyes behind her sunglasses.

She still could not help be angry at herself, especially after the way her relationship with Raymond turned out, that she had gone against her principles and had sex in his parents' house, something she felt guilty and disgusted about, something she would hate for her own daughter to do. It was disrespectful and in light of the breakup of her relationship with Raymond, the guilt had deepened into the anger she now felt against Raymond.

Not long after their first sexual encounter Ray told her that the day the both of them had the house completely to themselves was the day his parents had one of their major fights since the start of their divorce proceedings. That day his father was in Montego Bay preparing to fly back to the States while his mother was in Port Antonio with his grandmother and everyone seemed to be everywhere else, leaving the house in Stony Hill free for him to take his girlfriend home to have sex. The conversation that followed their love making that first time was mostly about him: that he would soon be moving out to his own apartment on the other side of New Kingston; that he was going to continue his law studies at University of the West Indies in Barbados and that he didn't need his parents, they needed him, and so on. Jayda never realized until now how emotionally vulnerable Raymond must have been but he hid it well. If he had been emotionally vulnerable because of his parents' broken marriage she had been emotionally vulnerable because she had opened up her heart, laid her emotions bare thinking she could trust the man who had taken her first flower of womanhood but who instead trampled all over that flowerbed. She had indeed believed that their love for each other was deepening the more they saw of each other, particularly after Raymond got the apartment in Mona and had more privacy, but she was soon to discover that the feelings of love had not been mutual but one-sided. She had loved him more than she thought a woman could ever love a man but he dusted her love aside. To him it was as inconsequential as a quick shower of summer rain.

"Look who's here!" Celia announced.

Jolted from her memories of the past, Jayda raised herself up on her elbows and stared through her sunglasses at Raymond as he stepped out of the wide open doorway from Celia's living room into the sunshine. He looked boyish in his white long-shorts and cool t-shirt, comfortable white moccasins on his feet.

She flushed, self-consciousness washing over her as he stepped toward her along the pool deck, smiling. He wore dark glasses so she could not tell exactly where his eyes focused, but from the tingling of the skin on her exposed legs she suspected his eyes probably roamed upward from her ankles to the tops of her thighs where her red high-cut bathing suit began. Instinctively she drew the soft gauzy floral print sarong around her waist to hide her thighs.

"Relaxing by the pool, Jayda?" he said. "Best place to be." He was carrying a plastic bag through which Jayda could make out the forms of large Bombay mangoes.

"Celia invited you?" Jayda asked, curious, especially after last night and the way he had showed up at the club.

"No. I called over at your place and your Aunt Vina told me where you were. Do you object?"

Jayda sat up and swung her legs off the sun chair. She was now fully upright and no longer relaxed or reposed.

"Not at all," she replied.

Celia strutted out into the sunshine, smiling, carrying a knife and a striped kitchen towel, and eyeing the mangoes in Raymond's plastic bag.

"Raymond, you couldn't do a better thing!" she exclaimed and grabbed the bag from him. "Plenty chairs around. Take the weight off your feet."

He drew up a chair close to Jayda while Celia pulled the mangoes out of the bag and placed them on the kitchen towel on the tiled floor beside her where she sat close to the edge of the pool.

"Last night was so loud and noisy we couldn't even get to talk," said Celia.

Jayda sat uncomfortably in her chair while Celia and Raymond led the small talk and ate their mangoes with gusto. Every now and then Jayda flicked her gaze sideways to look at Raymond. The way he sat there in his shorts eating the mango brought back to her so many images from the past; his boyishness, his zest and joy of life. He leaned his elbows on his knees and reached forward to prevent any mango pulp from soiling his shorts. Even as he and Celia swapped stories about local happenings, Jayda knew she still had his attention. He had not removed his glasses and from the tilt of his head she could tell when he observed her.

"I'm going to take these things into the house and leave you two alone," Celia said, rising from the edge of the pool and collecting the mango seeds, skins and kitchen towel inside the plastic bag.

Jayda stood up instantly and walked over to the shower unit alongside the pool area and tried to wash her hands without getting her whole body wet. Raymond came up behind her.

"Girl, you're looking good," he said. His voice was a low growl that only she could hear.

He washed his hands and followed her back to the sun chair where they dried their hands in both ends of a towel.

Jayda didn't know what to say to him. She didn't want him to see how ill at ease she was but the also didn't want to risk saying anything that might be misunderstood or just sound silly. She decided for the moment to say nothing.

"Natasha is here?" he asked, sitting down in the chair beside hers.

"Yes. She's with Celia's kids in the den."

He paused a moment before he spoke again.

"So what are you doing with yourself these days, Jayda?" he asked.

She answered him in the same brief manner she answered Victor.

"Do you have a steady guy?" he asked, removing his glasses. "Or was the guy at the club last night your boyfriend?"

"Which guy at the club?" she asked, pretending ignorance.

"The one who kissed you."

"That guy is not my boyfriend. He just took us all out to the club. He rents the efficiency at my parent's house."

"Oh yes. I think I've seen him before, very briefly when I passed by to see your aunt some time ago," Raymond said. "We all stay in touch you know. Not as much as we'd like because of schedules but Celia and Paul and some of the others from college, we keep in touch. We all miss Trevor, you know. Trevor was a tremendous guy. He was lucky to have someone like you, Jayda . . ."

Jayda bit her lips as he talked about Trevor and she could feel an aching in her heart and decided to change the subject immediately before she burst into tears. If they all missed Trevor, just think how much more she missed his presence, missed his touch in the night, missed his partnership in the parenting challenge with Natasha.

"Yes, Victor rents the efficiency," Jayda said quickly.

Ray looked silently at her, contemplating her posture, her slightly tense shoulders.

"Got a boyfriend back in the States?" he asked.

"No, Raymond, I don't. I make my own decisions. If I decide I don't want any hassles and heartaches with men right now, that is my decision."

"Are those your expectations, Jayda? That all you'll encounter are hassles and heartaches? You have no more hope?"

"I'm a hopeful person, Raymond. But right now I'm just hoping I can raise Natasha, make some money and live well. Down the road, if I meet a nice man, I meet a nice man. I'm not out there searching."

For one quiet moment Raymond gazed out at the shimmering blue water in the pool then he looked back at Jayda. "What about if there is a man out there looking for you?"

"I'll cross that bridge when I come to it."

"Are you willing to cross it now?" he asked earnestly, looking into her eyes.

Jayda smoothed back her braids from her face and looked away from him, averting her eyes upwards at the sunlight gleaming in the palm fronds overhead, the wind gusting soothingly.

"Raymond," she shook her head. "I don't understand you. After the way you treated me, threw my love aside like it was an old newspaper, telling me to my face that you are looking for Miss Right because I didn't fit the bill, how do you think I'm supposed to feel? How do you think I felt then? Humiliated, Raymond. People don't get over humiliation that easily. Humiliation lives with you and governs the way you think and feel about others."

"If you let it. It doesn't have to be that way. Anger can do that to people too . . . Look, Jayda. I'll be the first to admit that I was a selfish cock-of-the-walk back then. I didn't respect you as much as I should have. You were a respectable person, a beautiful, delicate young lady."

"You used me," Jayda flared, feeling herself getting angry.

"Jayda, I didn't use you. I really did like you. But you were moving too fast, and you were acting like you wanted to get married. That scared me. It's easier for me to admit now. Back then I never admitted to anyone that I could get scared."

"You ran away from me because you thought I wanted to get married?" Jayda was surprised.

"Yes," Raymond sat back and looked at her.

"Raymond, I had career plans I wanted to pursue. I wasn't thinking about marriage then. All I wanted was some kind of commitment."

"So what do you think commitment means—between a man and woman? The only way I would stop seeing other women was if I got married and settled down. I was too young to settle down and the signals you were giving me were that you wanted to settle down."

Jayda slowly took a deep breath and swallowed her rising anger, recognizing that they needed to talk, if for no other reason but to clear the air as civilized adults.

"Raymond, why in your search, have you come back around to me? How come all of a sudden, I'm Miss Right?"

"I'll be frank, Jayda. You've grown up. You grew up long before I did. You're even more beautiful than you were years ago, believe it or not—" He paused when he realized he'd made her smile. "Now I've grown up too. We match."

"Don't you have a girlfriend?" she asked.

"Not anyone steady."

"But women you have sex with anyway, right?"

"You don't mince words, do you?" he laughed.

"Do you mind my being direct?"

"No." He leaned forward slowly and looked steadily into her eyes. His face was much closer so hers now. He smelled shower-fresh and the dimples in his cheeks deepened as a mischievous thought surfaced to be vocalized. "Jayda, are you going to sit there and tell me you haven't been with a man since Trevor died?"

"That's right."

"But that's nearly three years."

"And I'm not ashamed, Ray. I'm not desperate either. And right now I'm not looking for a man. As I said I just want to take care of my daughter and myself. I'm thinking of going back to school too."

"Seems to me, Jayda, you're taking care of everything but your love life."

"I just don't want anymore heartaches. I had a wonderful relationship with Trevor. A great love life. In my life so far, every man I love seems to leave me. One walked out of my life. The other died. It's kind of scary. I don't want to go through anymore heartaches. My only consolation is that at least my father's still around. And I love him very much."

"So, Jayda, you would rather sentence yourself to a lonely life than take a chance with a man—namely me?"

A crisp mountain gust of air passing over the swimming pool made Jayda shudder and she pulled her sarong skirt tighter around her waist, even though the sun was still glaring hot. Perhaps it was the sensual way Raymond watched her that made her shiver.

"So why after all these years didn't your Miss Right materialize, Raymond?"

Raymond leaned back in his chair and stretched. He looked up at the sky while she studied his strong hairy legs stretched out before him. She looked away as soon as he looked at her.

"There were a couple of near misses," he said. "When I was living in America—in Philadelphia—I got engaged to a girl. We even had wedding plans. Then she got cold feet. She kept changing her mind back and forth until she discovered she was pregnant, then she really changed her mind and wanted us to have a real quick wedding but with all the expensive trimmings and so on. I was doubtful but I was willing to go along—for the child's sake. I wanted a kid. I realized I got to a stage in my life where I really wanted to be a dad. Then she had a miscarriage. The whole thing was one crazy emotional roller coaster. I don't think the woman was emotionally stable so I'm glad I didn't end up being married to her. The only regret I had and still have is the child that was lost, you know. A little boy." Raymond was silent for a moment and gazed off into the distance, his face totally serious for the first time since his arrival at Celia's house.

"A law practice in Florida caused me to leave Philly," he continued. "I was glad to get away from that woman's whining family. I took my Florida Bar exam, passed and went to work with a firm in Lauderhill. My father, who had remarried, came down from New York to live in Florida. He wasn't too far away from me. For a while I was like you, not wanting to get mixed up with anyone who might drain my emotions. I worked hard and undistracted for some time then I started partying again. No serious relationships, just unattached fun, but you can only have so much of that life before you get to the point when you need to prioritize. The scene started to get stale. I became a little frazzled. I guess you could say that's when I decided to move back to JA. My friends and even my dad tried to discourage me, citing crime and the economy as reasons not to return to the island but I'd had enough, at least for a while. I bought the house in Beverley Hills for my mom and my grandma. I have a house in Falmouth on the north coast which I lease out to a tourist timeshare contractor whenever I'm not using it."

"But you live in Beverley Hills?"

"Yes," he answered. "My parents' house in Stony Hill got sold off years ago."

"You've got it made," she murmured. "You just need a wife and kids."

"That's what I'm working on," a new smile warmed his face. He was close enough so that his index finger was able to touch her knee. She pulled away from him.

"Ray, that tickles," she said lightly. She sat back and heaved a sigh. "Ray, I didn't know I was going to hear your whole life story. I don't know if your intention in telling me all of this was to help me make up my mind about you, but somehow it doesn't help me at all. I'm a woman with my own agendas, with a daughter to raise, with a life of my own to live—"

"Listen, Jayda. I made a mistake when I gave you up. I realize that now . . ."

"Maybe it was no mistake, Ray. It worked out that way for a reason. Hind-sight is always twenty-twenty and never needs glasses!"

They both laughed.

*

Jayda spent two days with Trevor's family in the hills of Clarendon, a slower pace of life, tranquility and country folk.

Living for a while with the folk who woke at the crack of dawn, harvested coffee and planted callalloo, she had a chance to reflect on her life and reflect on a man who'd unveiled the wellspring of her passion. She could not get his face out of her mind, the way it looked as he spoke to her beside the pool at Celia's house as he told her how he'd made a mistake when he'd given her up. After their talk he didn't stay long at the house. He left just before Celia, Jayda and the children sat down for Sunday dinner. His stopping by Celia's house to see Jayda had been a teaser, a deliberate rouse to start Jayda thinking about him again and all the possibilities that presented themselves to her.

She couldn't understand why she had been so angry at Raymond before. Was she angry because her initial plans fifteen years ago had not gone the way of her dreams and she ended up marrying Trevor instead of him? She studied that question over and over again and realized the irrationality of it. Fifteen years ago, despite the heat and the passion, she and Raymond were emotionally mismatched, and had she married him the probability of her ending up a divorcee instead of a widow was much greater. Not that either of these options would be appealing to anyone. Looking back she realized it indeed had been that way for a reason. "Nothing never done before the time", the old country folks would say.

She could not have done any better than marrying Trevor when she did. He was a gentle, quiet man, unselfish, though with a tendency to be inhibited. There has been moments when she ached for his attention and he failed to recognize her need. Trevor was more of a cerebral personality while she tended to be more physical. Nevertheless Trevor was a man who enjoyed his life before he got sick. Walking in the hills Jayda had a chance to embrace her memories and regroup her emotions before

Once back in town by midweek she went shopping with Aunt Vina. The following day Celia drove her around to visit some of their old college friends, some at their homes, others at their jobs. With the children, Celia and Jayda drove everywhere and at one point stopped at Hellshire Beach to eat up some fried fish and *festival*, and wade in the water.

Thursday evening was quiet. Jayda sat on the terrace in a sun chair reading the latest copy of Ebony and sipping a glass of Hawaiian Punch. Suddenly Victor appeared beside her. His aftershave preceded him so she was not startled by his sudden appearance. He walked past her and leaned against the balustrade of the terrace, folded his arms in front of him and stared at her, a smile on his face.

"Hi, Jayda. How you doing?" His baritone voice was rich and clear on this quiet sultry evening.

"Fine," she replied, awkwardly. She would have preferred to remain by herself. She was wearing shorts and she could feel his eyes roving the length of her nude legs.

"So how's the real estate business in Miami?" he asked casually.

"It has its ups and downs. But I'm not in it anymore, real estate I mean. Ever since my husband died, I kind of lost interest."

"So what do you do now?"

"I work as an assistant at a law firm in Fort Lauderdale. It puts food on my table."

"So does my boring job," Victor laughed and unfolded his arms. He straightened up and turned to face the view of the mountainside, his back halfway to her.

"You don't like being an accountant?"

He turned his face to her over his shoulder and replied, "Sure. But one day I want to be my own boss. Run my own business, not be running for Mr. Big, whoever he is. I'll be Mr. Big."

"Ambitious," Jayda said, and idly flipped the pages of her magazine.

"You like an ambitious man?" he asked turning fully to face her, his elbows resting on the top of the balustrade, the top buttons of his striped blue shirt open.

"Yes, but one who's realistic. One who works hard to achieve his goals, not just sit back and think success will come to him simply by talking about it."

"I consider myself realistic," Victor said and walked away from the balustrade. He approached Jayda and took a seat in the upright sun chair beside her. "For instance, realistically, I know if I want a woman like you, I'd have to work darned hard to get you. You are not a simple woman. You are devastatingly attractive, may I be so bold as to say . . . sexy!" He paused as though waiting for her to say Thank You, but Jayda said nothing. She averted her eyes, her awareness of him intensifying. She was flattered but somehow having Victor come on to her this strongly simply was not in the picture. Especially since now she could feel the icebergs melting inside her whenever she thought about Raymond. If she were still fighting her feelings for Raymond then this flirtation with Victor would certainly be a delightfully strategic diversion. Victor certainly was not a bad looking man. She knew some of her friends back in Miami would consider him quite a hunk, especially those who went for guys whose looks combined African lips and European eyes.

Victor leaned forward, his elbows on his knees as he stared into her eyes.

"I know a guy on the North Coast who has a boat. A big boat, actually a yacht, parked up in a marina in Montego Bay. I was thinking it might be a good idea if we took an excursion to the north coast and meet this guy with the yacht. Actually I have already spoken to him. He's going to be having a party on board this weekend. Before you say no, hear me out. I already told Celia about it and she thinks its a great idea but she says you probably won't go without your good mutual friend Raymond."

"Good God! What a woman love to meddle!" Jayda shook her head and put her face in her hand.

"She told me about you and this guy," Victor said.

"I wish she'd stay out of my business. Truly."

"Don't worry. She didn't give me any intimate secrets but that's how come I know that if I was to have a woman like you I'd have to work hard. But not to worry. This would be a group excursion. Adults only though. If you and Celia could leave the kids at home that would be good, don't you think?"

In the midst of her confused thoughts Jayda actually found herself liking the idea.

"So who would be going?"

"You, Celia, myself of course. Raymond if he wants to come along. Your cousin from England—Brandon."

"Is Raymond officially invited?"

"Yes."

"Are you inviting him directly or through me? He might not come if he's not directly invited."

"I would prefer if he didn't come, but your cupid Celia would give us all a hard time so he is invited. If you want you can give me his phone number so I can call him myself."

"No. It's all right. It probably won't be necessary for you to do that," Jayda said.

"Because he would come no matter what, as long as you are there, right?" Jayda didn't respond, not wanting to dignify the sarcasm in his voice.

*

They left Kingston early Friday morning in an eight-seater mini-van, Victor at the wheel. The dark sky hadn't yet given birth to the sun as they drove into mountainous terrain cutting across the island's mid-section to get to the north coast.

The 110-foot yacht was magnificent. It was owned by an American businessman who chartered it out frequently. The man who was having the party was a Jamaican banker who had chartered it to entertain out of town guests but it wasn't the banker who actually invited Victor and his friends. The banker's associate was related to the man who Victor worked for in Kingston. Jayda and the others checked into a hotel and prepared for the party on the yacht.

They all looked fine. Jayda was excited, despite herself. Raymond did not look as handsome at any other time in his life as he did now. He was more mature, self assured, relaxed and downright sexy in his dark shirt and well-tailored slacks, broad firm shoulder muscles rippling beneath the soft dark fabric. Eyes shining. He smelled good, and tonight he looked totally desirable.

For Jayda, the deep awesome desire she felt for him years ago came flooding back now, overwhelming her. Deep down she was afraid, afraid because if Raymond did nothing more than breathe into her ear she would give herself to him. Tonight. And if she gave herself to him she would be setting herself up for more hurt, more heartache. Over and over again she kept telling herself there was no way she could give her heart to this man to let him to break it a second time.

Jayda shared a hotel room with Celia. Celia seemed to be taking forever to get herself ready for the party. By around seven o'clock Raymond called their room to see if Jayda was ready. He arranged to meet Jayda in the bar downstairs where they could wait until everyone was ready for the drive to the marina. Raymond had gotten a room for himself while Victor shared with Brandon.

Raymond sat at the end of the bar close to the entrance, and the moment he saw Jayda he stood up and approached her. Walking her back to the bar he said,

"You look so beautiful tonight." His eyes moved down from the top of her head all the way to her feet and back up again, this time his eyes meeting hers.

She wore a slinky red gown with boot-lace shoulder straps encrusted with rhinestones that revealed much of her smooth brown shoulders and curvy cleavage. She fingered her smooth braids that curled under at her shoulders. Moderate make-up enhanced her beautiful facial features. As Ray took her hand in his, he slid his other arm around her waist and led her to the bar.

"Cheers!" Raymond toasted her with a glass of wine.

Jayda lifted her own glass. "Cheers."

"This is turning out better than I thought," Raymond said.

"In what way?"

"I have to admit, I had my doubts about coming. I don't like that guy Victor. Too shifty for my liking."

"You were afraid he would make a move on me?" Jayda joked.

"That too . . . Jayda, you probably still don't believe how serious I am about making it work this time. You and I. This is no play-play thing this time. This is the real thing."

Jayda said nothing, sipping her wine and listening to the piano player in the corner of the room.

Celia, Victor and Jayda's cousin Brandon soon arrived.

"Shall we go?" said Victor, jingling the van keys.

Victor parked the van inside the secured parking lot at the marina and the group made its way to the area where the yacht was berthed. People in shimmering party clothes and fine jewelry milled around on the dock, talking and laughing. Some people were already standing on the yacht's upper deck.

Jayda, with the others, entered the main salon, a large brightly lit room with mirrors and small arc lights. She guessed there couldn't have been more than fifty guests. The music was already playing in the main lounge, and people were drinking and sitting around talking. Not too many were dancing yet.

Suddenly a young woman walked up to Raymond, scintillating in a low-cut sequin blouse and tight black pants. She was almost as tall as Ray, slender and shapely with light brown skin and flowing long slightly-frizzed hair and green eyes. When she closed in on him she pushed her arm through his.

"Raymond, honey! What a long time I haven't seen you." She planted a kiss on his cheek.

Up to now the woman hadn't even looked at Jayda who had her arm threaded through Raymond's other arm.

Raymond lost his composure and looked from Jayda to the young woman and back again.

"Raymond, cha! How you stay so!" the young woman pressed him.

"Do I know you?" he asked, looking back at her.

She raised one of her long slender arms and ran her fingers through her hair and tossed her long black tresses away from her face.

"Course you know Candy Besson. That's me. Why do men have such a short memory?"

"Well this man has a long memory. And I don't remember you . . . Meet Jayda. She's a very good friend of mine."

Jayda could feel anger welling up inside her. Who was this ill-mannered hussy? And why was Raymond acting like he didn't know her?

"Hi," Jayda said quickly and quietly and was about to move away from Raymond when he caught her arm and held it tightly as he told Candy to have a nice evening.

When they were alone again, Jayda relaxed a little but the glitz of the evening was already tarnished.

"You were always a very popular guy," Jayda commented.

"If I was a betting man, I would bet that right about now you are thinking that Miss Candy was one of my ships that passed in the night."

"Possibly." Jayda said.

"You mean possibly *I'm right about what you're thinking* or possibly *Miss Candy was one of my passing ships?*"

"Any way you care to take it, Raymond." Jayda shrugged her shoulders and looked away from him. She studied the sumptuous decor of the yacht's main salon where the party was still in the talk-and-socialize stage. Miss Candy Besson seemed to know several other people there, including Victor whom she chatted with briefly before moving on. Hors d'oeuvres and cocktails were served. There were some high-powered business types, walking around with cellular phones as well as cocktail glasses. An hour later the yacht sailed out from the dock. It would drop anchor a few miles out while the party heated up.

Coming up to midnight the party indeed began to heat up. The music got louder, got raucous. The social chit-chatting gave way to dancing and shouts of laughter.

After a hot exciting time on the dance floor, Raymond led Jayda outside to a quiet part of the deck where they stood and looked at the lights twinkling on the shoreline. Raymond stood behind her and put his arms around her. She pressed her back against him as he surrounded her with his arms and rested the side of his face upon the crown of her head. She took his large hands and caressed his fingers, slowly, self-consciously at first then she brought his hands to rest on her breasts. She had now given him the green light to touch her intimately. Without anymore prompting his hands continued to massage her breasts, discreetly, under the cover of his arms as he held her from behind. Slowly he turned her around to face him. He stroked the sides of her face with his hands and found her lips. She could feel his breath hot on her face as his mouth sought hers, as his lips imprisoned hers in a long kiss that caused the tide of passion to roll in, spraying all the memories into the present to overwhelm her like waves rolling in to crash on a beach. She had been a lonely beach. He was the wave that came crashing in upon that lonely beach. Unable to stop a groan from rising in her throat she tried to push him away but he wouldn't let her go.

"Please stop, Ray," she breathed against his cheek. "People will see us."

"I don't care. Let everyone see . . ."

Several other revelers had come out to talk and gaze upon the lights on the shoreline or perhaps to indulge in a physical moment the way Jayda and Raymond were doing. At that moment, Jayda thought she recognized Victor's voice amidst the other murmuring voices. His voice stopped suddenly. Jayda glanced briefly around Ray's shoulder in time to see Victor step quickly back through the door and into the salon.

Later, Jayda met up with Celia in the restroom. Celia was in high spirits. It seemed she couldn't stop laughing. Her gold loop earrings shimmered against her cheeks as she gave a wide-mouthed grin. She seemed to laugh at everything. Jayda suspected she was high on something other than wine. In fact, as Celia leaned in closer to Jayda to exchange some idle gossip, Jayda could smell a weed on her breath that was not tobacco. Celia played like a single woman, like a woman without a care in the world, no husband, no children. She partied harder now than in the days when she really was a single woman, Jayda thought. Celia had better watch out because playing as hard as she did certainly wasn't going to win her any points in her marriage, even though her husband was always away on business, but who knew: wherever he was he was probably playing as hard as she was. What kind of a marriage was theirs? Jayda didn't want to know the answer. All she was certain of was that she would rather live alone with only herself and her child than live in a marriage like Celia's.

While in the rest room, Celia updated Jayda on how her evening had been so far.

"Jayda, girl! I must persuade Paul to save up and invest in a yacht, man! I could sell the house and live on a thing like this forever!"

"And where would the kids go school?" Jayda asked as she took her powder compact from her bag and began patting the shine off her nose. There wasn't much elbow room in the tiny space in front of the mirror where Celia tried to cram herself to apply more lipstick.

"You're such a killjoy, Jayda! You're always so practical, it's almost boring! Aren't you having fun?"

"Of course I'm having fun."

"You and Baby Ray look so good together, child!"

"Well, I paid a lot for this dress," Jayda said. After she put her compact away she too began to apply lipstick.

Jayda collided with Victor upon emerging from the restroom moments later.

"Hello, beautiful," he smiled, his eyes fastened upon her. "This is the first time since the evening began that I've had a chance to tell you how wonderful you look. Boy, if I was the one in there with a chance to have you, I'd be the luckiest man.

He took the tips of her fingers in his hands and raised up her arm as he demonstratively admired her, trying to get her to twirl around but she didn't move. A slow song was playing.

"You don't think your friend would mind too much if I asked you for a dance?" he said.

"It's nothing to do with my friend, Victor, but I really don't feel like dancing."

"Aw come on," he insisted. "Since he's not around, can't I just sneak in one little dance?"

At that moment the song changed and with it the tempo, a thumping R&B number that Jayda heard played on Miami radio stations all the time.

"All right," she said finally. "Let's dance." She was now reassured there would be no body contact since this was going to be a more upbeat dance.

When the song was through Victor took her by the elbow and led her off the dance floor. "Let's look for your friend. Can't leave you on your own. Another man might want to take you over."

Jayda looked at him askance, puzzled by his facetious tone.

"I don't seem to see your friend," Victor said, looking about.

"Don't worry about it," Jayda said casually.

"Isn't this a fantastic yacht!" he exclaimed. "One of these days when I'm my own boss, I'd like to be able to charter something like this. Maybe even own one. Sail up and down the coast. Maybe sail to the Cayman Islands or Bermuda . . . . So you're having a good time, Jayda?" he continued conversationally as they walked down a narrow passage leading off from the main salon where it was quieter.

"Yes, a very good party," Jayda replied.

"I'm glad you came. I'll never forget the way you look tonight . . ."

Jayda began to look at Victor with suspicion. She wondered if he was trying to get her into one of the cabins so he could force himself on her. There were two doors in the passage which Jayda suspected led to cabins. Victor suddenly grasped her hand and pulled her to him.

"Victor, what are you doing!"

He opened the door to the cabin marked "B".

"I don't want to go in there with you. You're too out of order!" she shouted.

"I thought I heard voices," he said as quickly as he opened the door. The lights were on inside the room, a bright champagne-colored room with shiny chrome fittings and dark chintz curtains. Jayda was about to pull away from Victor and his sordid advances when the scene inside the cabin filled her eyes and brought pain to her heart. Her limbs weakened and she almost stumbled back against Victor.

Candy Besson, her long hair spread out on her shoulders, was leaning back against a pillow on one of the beds, her head tilted backwards, her knees drawn up and spread apart, still wearing her tight black pants and high heeled shoes. She looked like she was crying but Jayda wasn't sure. Leaning down over her, one knee on the bed, was Raymond.

"I knew it was too good to be true!" Jayda yelled. "Too damn good!"

"Jayda, it's not what you think!" Raymond released the girl immediately and jumped up. He took a step back from the bed and spread his hands. "Believe me, Jayda. It's not what you think."

Jayda dashed out of the cabin, almost knocking Victor off balance. Raymond came after her, shoving Victor out the way. Jayda could hear Victor's cry of alarm.

"Come here, Jayda, let's talk," Raymond said, pulling her back by the elbow.

Seething with anger and venom she yanked back her arm from him.

"Leave me alone. I'm glad I found you out before it was too late. Before I started trusting you again. I don't want to see you anymore. You haven't changed. J-just get out of my life, you hear!" She stormed off and plowed her way through the crowded dance floor, her vision blurred by tears, tears she had not wanted Ray to see. She emerged on the other side of the dance floor and escaped out the door to the deck where the fresh sea wind smacked her in the face. The vista of the twinkling lights on the shore no longer held any magic for her. Not now. She just wished she were on dry land so that she could return to the hotel and lock herself into the hotel room and cry and scream at herself for having been such a fool at being taken in once more by the wily charms of Raymond Fennerman. How could she have been so stupid as to believe he could have changed. He was setting her up for another heartache. She was almost ensnared like a naive rabbit caught in a trap to be cooked and devoured. She found him out just in time but she still could not squelch the feelings of humiliation. She had allowed him to touch her intimately on this same deck some time earlier that evening. They had kissed and her searing hot passion for him had returned only to be dashed back in her face like scalding oil. Oh God, the humiliation, the pain. She couldn't stand it. How was she going to tolerate the remaining few hours on board the yacht before the return to shore? Was there nowhere to hide? She didn't want to run into Ray again.

She tried to find Celia.

Celia was dancing with a man and smoking a cigarette. They were on the dance floor near the bar area. Jayda would not have interrupted under normal circumstances but this time she needed to speak with Celia. Celia seductively pried herself out of the man's arms and promised him she'd be back.

When Jayda dragged her out on the deck and told her what had happened Celia was shocked. She suddenly seemed stone cold sober.

"I don't believe what I'm hearing," she said.

"Well believe it. This whole evening has turned into a shambles for me. If I could swim back to shore I would. So help me! I want a cabin. I wonder who I could see?"

"You're asking me?" Celia's eyes widened. "Ask Victor, he knows these people . . . No, wait. I think I know the woman who might help. She's the wife of the man who threw the party tonight. I get around, you know. I get to know the players. Nice woman. Let's find her and ask the question."

The woman was Mrs. Lu-Chin, tall, buxom, brown and elegant in a close-fitting floral calf-length gown and high heels, her shiny black hair brushed back into a large bun. She looked as though she might have been in her fifties. She became instantly concerned about Jayda, fearing Jayda might be sea sick but Jayda told her she had a thumping headache and would appreciate if she could lay down in an empty cabin. There were only four guest cabins on board, Lu-Chin explained and the only one not taken was the cabin she personally used and kept locked.

"Come this way." She led Jayda and Celia to the "stateroom" as Mrs. Lu-Chin called it and unlocked the door. It was quite spacious and was filled with gift-boxes and slinky gowns on hangers. "Let me clear off this bed. No one will bother you in here. We should be going back to shore in the next couple of hours. We'll come and get you when we dock."

*

By two a.m. Jayda was sitting in the van on the dock, waiting for Brandon and Celia. She even tolerated Victor's cigarette smoke as he waited behind the wheel. Still drowsy, Jayda leaned back in her seat behind Victor, head against the head-rest. Jayda hadn't seen Raymond since she emerged from the cabin and came ashore. She suspected he had no plans to ride back to the hotel in the van with her and the others. He'd most likely make his own way back.

"Where's Celia?" Jayda whined. "I'm tired. I want to get back to the hotel."

Victor didn't answer right away but after a moment he said,

"I'm really sorry your evening got spoilt like that. True. It's a damn crying shame, man."

"None of your concern," Jayda said coldly. "Where is that damn Celia, man! I'm starting to get real annoyed now. Victor, why don't you drop me off at the hotel now and then come back for Celia? I mean, where could she be? I'm sure nearly everybody's off the boat by now."

At that moment Celia appeared at the top of the gang-way and half staggered down it. Brandon was behind her, helping her make her way down. He'd been sent to look for her. A cigarette dangled at the corner of Celia's mouth and her eyes rolled.

Victor instantly started the engine.

Celia was mumbling and cussing as Brandon loaded her on board and she flopped into the passenger seat beside Victor.

As the engine revved she took the cigarette out of her mouth and looked back into the van. Her eyes focused on Jayda.

"Jayda, honey, you all right?"

Jayda didn't answer.

"Where is Raymond?" Celia asked.

"Raymond not here," Victor said.

"I can see that. But why he's not here? This night shouldn't end like this man. I'm not making it end like this. I getting to the bottom of this!"

"Celia, you don't see how Jayda tired? She just wants to get back to the hotel and sleep," said Victor, irritated.

"I just don't like how this whole thing spoil-up so, man!" Celia fell back against the seat as Victor stepped on the gas, and gunned the van out of the parking lot.

At the hotel, Jayda went immediately upstairs to the hotel room, leaving Celia hanging around in the lobby with Victor. Both Celia and Victor seemed to be hankering after the bar for another drink but it was likely the hotel bar was already closed. Jayda didn't care. She just wanted to be alone.

*

Jayda didn't awake until around eight-thirty the next morning as the sunlight spilled through the white mesh curtains at the windows. She turned over and glanced across at the other bed. It was empty, the sheets rolled back. At least Celia had slept there last night. Jayda suddenly heard water running in the adjoining bathroom. She lay down again and looked up at the sun-dappled ceiling. Suddenly the events of last night came rushing back to her and she wanted to roll over and pull the blankets over her head.

At that moment Celia appeared from the bathroom, wearing only a bra and matching panties, her plump yellow-brown thighs rubbing together.

"You're awake," she said.

Jayda yawned and sat up.

"If we leave Montego Bay later than nine, we won't be back in Kingston till nearly nightfall," Jayda complained.

"I'm not driving back with Victor," Celia said and sat down on her bed across from Jayda.

"Why?"

"Because if I do, I'm going to kill him. And if I kill him, we'll all end up dead because he's the one driving."

Jayda sat bolt upright in bed, urging Celia with her eyes to hurry up and say what she had to say.

"Jayda, you know that Raymond left from six o'clock this morning. Front desk said he checked out and took a taxi to the airport. The guy is already back in Kingston."

A painful sinking feeling attacked Jayda's stomach and the hurt of last night returned with intensity.

"Why don't you want to drive back with Victor?" Jayda asked, trying to tear her mind away from Raymond.

"Jayda," Celia leaned back on her hands. "Did you know that the whole thing last night was a set-up? A blasted set-up?"

"What do you mean?"

"I mean I hope you didn't cuss off Raymond too harshly. He was set-up, girl!" Celia said emphatically. "You know that girl Candy Besson? You want to know who she is? Victor's cousin! I buck-up on her last night. Girl was as drunk as a bat, crying and weeping like a damn fool down in the lobby after you came up. She said she was sorry she did what she did but was only playing the game for Victor. Victor invited her on the trip only if she agreed to set-up Raymond, get you to walk in on them and destroy whatever good thing you and Raymond was trying to make. I honestly don't see how Victor could have possibly seen himself filling Raymond's shoes if Raymond was to walk out of your life. If Victor's plan never backfired he figured he would step right into Raymond's shoes and try to have you."

Jayda put her face in her hand and shook her head. She couldn't even begin to described the feelings coursing through her right now. All she knew was she wanted to die.

"A set-up? But why?" she lifted her head and stared into space.

"Jayda, you're an idiot if you don't see why. That Victor is a dirty pig. He wanted you so he played a dirty trick to get you. Fortunately, his cousin's a drunken fool and I got to hear the whole story. She said she got Raymond on his own, then pretended she was sick so that he would help her to the cabin. Then of course Victor brought you in for the finale."

"Does Victor know that you know?"

"Yes! I went to his room and cussed him out! He didn't want me to tell you of course, but what does he expect me to do? Keep my mouth shut and pretend his dirty tricks don't stink!"

Jayda remembered how Victor effectively led her to that cabin last night. At the time however, she had believed he was trying to get her alone to seduce her. All the time he knew the set-up was in place and all he wanted was for Jayda to catch Raymond in a compromising situation. And Jayda had fallen for the trick, believing that Raymond was no good. The pain of the heartbreak from fifteen years ago was still with her, controlling her mind and her heart. She hadn't let go of that pain, even after all those years, after being married to Trevor, having a career, having a child and getting on with her life in Florida. She thought she'd been getting on with her life. Now she realized that the pain of years ago was still very much a part of her. She had listened to the voice of Pain and it told her not to believe in anyone, not to love again. She had judged Raymond even before she'd given him the chance to tell his side of the story. She now realized her mistake. What a fool she'd been. She remembered Raymond's earnest plea to talk with her last night but she pulled herself away and wouldn't listen. She hid herself away until the party was over then she came ashore.

Today he was gone.

Jayda started to bawl with remorse, like the hurt young school girl of years ago. Celia came and sat down beside her and hugged her.

"Come on, Jayda. Let's forget it. Come on now. Pull yourself together."

"I don't want to ride home with Victor either," Jayda sobbed.

"Did you bring much money with you? If you did, then we could both do what Raymond did and fly back."

Jayda tried to compose herself and Celia released her.

"Celia, I didn't come with lots of money. Taking a plane back to Kingston was definitely not in the picture when I got in Victor's van to come here for the party. I have enough to pay for my room and breakfast and maybe a souvenir but that's it. And what about Brandon."

"Brandon can drive back with Victor."

"No! Brandon's my cousin. You think I could just leave him like that?"

Celia thought for a moment. "I might call Bev and have her wire me something. I don't have a red cent." Bev was Celia's sister.

"Why don't we take a jitney?" said Jayda.

"If you think Victor's van would take a whole day to get to Kingston, then a jitney with all the stops and starts and twisting and turning and market women with baskets would take a whole day and a night and a day again before we got to Kingston."

*

Jayda had to swallow her anger and her pride to be able to tolerate the ride back with Victor. He was very apologetic to Jayda and before the journey began tried to engage her in a conversation to explain why he did what he did but Celia loudly shut him up and reminded him he ought to be ashamed of himself. After that he never spoke directly to Jayda or Celia again for the rest of the journey.

They did not get back to Kingston until after six-thirty in the evening as the sky reddened and hunger rumbled in their stomachs, even though Victor had driven like a madman along the high mountain roads, meandering above treacherous gorges and ravines. The only person to speak to Victor was Brandon. Victor was not in a talkative mood, and he would frequently look at Jayda through the rear view mirror. Sitting in one of the seats behind him she could feel his eyes on her and she decided to go and stretch out in the long seat at the back of the van. Victor honked rudely at people in the streets who flagged him down believing the vehicle to be a public minibus. He zoomed by, leaving them in the dust and some of the people in tiny mountain hamlets cussed after him. Other than that, and a few times when it seemed the van came dangerously close to the edge of a ravine, the journey back was uneventful.

At around seven-thirty that evening, Jayda met Natasha on the steps of her parents' house and gave her a hug. Aunt Vina waited on the steps with smiles and hugs. Celia greeted her children also and decided not to hang around but to take them straight home.

"How was the trip?" asked Vina, nudging Jayda and smiling.

"A disaster."

"What?" The smile disappeared from Vina's face.

"I don't want to talk about it right now, Auntie. I need a shower real bad. And some food to eat."

Later that evening Jayda relaxed in her bedroom alone. She oiled and massaged her scalp and brushed away the tears on her cheeks. She would be leaving for the States in a few days. She needed to apologize to Raymond before she left. She must admit to her mistake and ask for no hard feelings. Forget forgiveness. In the short space of time since her return to Jamaica she and Ray hadn't bonded that much where this dispute should require her asking for *forgiveness.* She picked up the extension in her room and dialed his number at the house in Beverley Hills. His mother answered the phone.

"He's not here right now, you know, Jayda," she said quietly. "So I'm not going to be seeing you before you go back? How come you haven't visited yet? Raymond told me you were here, but you and I aren't strangers. You must come and see me before you go." Jayda could picture Mrs. Fennerman's little cupid's-bow lips as she spoke. "When are you coming to visit?"

"I have been busy, up and down. I was in Clarendon last week."

Mrs. Fennerman asked about Jayda's parents before concluding the call by saying that when Raymond returned she would give him the message that Jayda had called.

Jayda hung up. Just then she heard Vina's voice in the hall at the top of the stairs, calling her.

"Jayda, you have a visitor!"

"But I'm in my nightie!" Jayda called back. She opened the door and looked out. Her aunt was on the landing poised to go back down stairs.

"It's Raymond. He's downstairs. He said he stopped by to make sure you got back safely—" Vina suddenly turned and came back up the stairs and along the hall towards Jayda. "I thought Raymond went with you to this trip."

"He did but he never came back with me. He flew back. It's a long story. I can't tell you now."

"I like long stories," said Vina. "You can tell me later after he's gone."

Jayda changed into a plain beige chemise dress, a pair of sandals. She moistened her lips with some Chapstick, and went downstairs. She could hear laughter and someone messing around on the piano in the living room. When Jayda went in she saw Raymond and Natasha tapping out chaotic notes on the piano keys and Vina standing with her hands on her hips, watching them. Brandon was lounging in the sofa, his legs stretched out before him, a can of beer in his hands.

Raymond straightened as she appeared. His eyes steadied on her and a smile played at the corner of his lips. Then his teeth showed as he opened his mouth to greet her.

"Hi, Jayda," Raymond said. "How are you?" He looked cool and comfortable in a loose white cotton shirt over dark cotton slacks and loafers.

"I'm fine," she said awkwardly. She didn't feel like shouting over the din of the piano. "Do you mind if we go into the kitchen?"

"OK," he said. "Brandon, show Natasha how to play Ragga-Ragga on that thing!"

"You want a drink now, Raymond?" asked Vina.

"No. I won't be stopping long. As I said, I just came by to see if Jayda was OK."

Vina went back into the living room as Jayda led Raymond to the kitchen. She could feel that sad sinking feeling in her stomach again, but this time it was tinged with hope.

"I called your house a little while ago. Your mother said you were out."

"Yeh . . ." He suddenly appeared awkward too.

They stood beside the large dining table. Jayda turned to him and looked up into his eyes.

"Look, Raymond. I owe you an apology . . ."

"Shhh." Raymond stepped closer and gently put his index finger against her lips. Then he took her by the shoulders and pressed her to him, squeezing her tightly. "Nothing or nobody is going to stop this train," he whispered against her hair. "Nobody. God's given me a second chance. It was a pity my good friend Trevor had to pass away and leave you a widow. It's a pity that as Natasha's father he won't be around anymore to watch her grow up. There are a lot of things that are negative, but for me there is a positive side to all of this . . . And that's my second chance." He cupped her cheeks in his large hands and tilted her face up to his and covered her mouth with his lips. "I love you, Jayda. I don't just want you. I need you. In my life I always thought I wanted things. I worked hard, made money and I got the things I wanted. Sometimes the things you need are not always easy to get . . . I was thinking about a lot of things on the plane ride back to Kingston. I shouldn't have left you."

"No, Raymond, I was wrong. I judged you," Jayda shook her head and held him away from herself a moment. "I was still living in the past, too afraid to trust anyone anymore. If Celia had never found out the truth of what happened, I would have gone back to America thinking the worst of you. And Raymond, even if we are just ordinary friends, that wouldn't be fair still, would it?"

"I don't want us to be ordinary friends, Jayda . . ." Raymond said. "I want us to be more than friends."

His words brought a memory echoing back from the past, the same sentiments she had. Jayda put her arms around him and melted into him, longing for his touch, for his kisses, succumbing to the willingness to give herself to him totally. She wanted him with an indescribable passion that seared her flesh, scorched her limbs, burned in her soul. She searched for his lips and found them, firm, hot, possessive lips. Her own heartbeat and his combined was deafening to the point where they hadn't even heard the sound on the far side of the kitchen leading to the back porch and the efficiency where Victor lived. They never saw Victor as he was about to enter the cool, spotless kitchen but stopped and retreated when he saw them embracing each other in the quiet dining room.

*

It was like being awakened after a long, long sleep; like thirst being quenched after a long dry walk without water, an undeniable sense of renewal.

Jayda and Raymond had found each other again. Two days before Jayda was due to return to Florida, Raymond took her out for a drive and a drink at the Morgan's Harbor Beach Club where they talked and reminisced about the old days. Raymond talked with affection about Trevor and Jayda hadn't realized until now how close the two men had been in boyhood.

In the purple twilight, they walked hand in hand around the marina and gazed out at the lights on the shoreline across the harbor. The twinkling lights in the range of mountains above the city reflected on the harbor waters. Jayda and Ray talked and talked, not wanting to part for the evening.

They decided to check into the hotel as Mr. and Mrs. Fennerman.

"I don't have a tooth-brush or fresh underwear," Jayda protested.

"I'll buy you a travel kit from the gift shop tomorrow morning. It has everything you'll need for your morning hygiene routine."

"We shouldn't be doing this, Ray. Really. We're not teenagers anymore."

"Which is why I know for sure—now more than at any other time—that I want to be doing this with you. The time is right, Miss Right."

Jayda grinned at him through the sultry evening light that settled in over the marina and the harbor.

"Lady, I want you," he whispered as he took her in his arms and kissed her once the door was closed and he had her all to himself in their clean, quiet hotel room overlooking the calm waters of the harbor.

His desire for her brought a sense of renewal to Jayda. She was renewed by his every touch as he slowly and carefully undressed her and lay her down on the bed; by his every move as he penetrated her body with his between the soft white sheets. The lovers were concealed away from the outside world, from family and friends. Just the two of them in their own world filled with a deep satisfying joy as they pleasured each other to an awesome ecstacy. Raymond covered her lips with his, covered her neck and breasts with hot kisses and Jayda succumbed, holding him tightly as though there was nothing else in the world but him to hold on to. Complete and utter surrender weakened her and left her blissfully drained as she lay back against the pillow and felt him touch her softly, intimately, reacquainting himself with her, not wanting to let her go.

*

In the morning he disappeared only to return with bags of items he purchased at the hotel gift store, toothpaste, toothbrushes, a colorful sarong beach dress for her.

"I hope it's the right size," he said as Jayda marveled at the beauty of the outfit and held it against her body while looking in the mirror.

Breakfast was delivered to their room and they ate it on the balcony overlooking the harbor, now blue and glassy in the placid morning light.

"If things had gone according to my secret plan we would have done this at my house in Falmouth," Raymond said and took a sip of coffee.

"What do you mean?" Jayda asked.

"I had wanted you and me to drive to Falmouth after the party on the yacht and spend some time at the place I was telling you about. At the moment it's vacant, no time-share tourists around. From the onset I had no intention of us driving back with Victor and Celia. I wanted us to go our separate ways and make our own way back to Kingston, but as it turned out . . ."

"The rest is history," Jayda finished his sentence for him and looked out at the bright sheen on the water below them.

"And this . . ." he said, leaning to one side, resting his elbow on the arm of the sun chair as he reached into the pocket of his shorts. He pulled out a small navy blue box and held it delicately between thumb and forefinger and presented it to her across the table.

Jayda's heart skipped a beat. It couldn't be what she thought it was. It couldn't be! She hesitated before taking it. Carefully opening the plush little box she stared down at the gleaming diamond ring, embedded in the soft dark velvet cushion.

"It's a ring!" she exclaimed.

"That's right."

"B-but why? Are you proposing to me, Ray? You know I can't—I just can't—!" She found herself lost for words. Then she said, "Ray, I'm here on a short vacation. I'm almost ready to go back to Florida. This just is not—"

"Jayda," he whispered and took her hands across the table. "Put on the ring, baby. Try it on. I want you to think about it. I want you to think about what the ring means. I don't want an answer right now."

"But, Ray, I can't do this. It's too sudden. And what about Natasha? Children can be . . . very funny about things."

"Natasha is a sweet child, just like her mother. And she has a lot of her father in her too. And I could not have had a better friend than Trevor. I'd never force her to love me, nor would I try to buy her love. But I think she'll be my friend, especially when she sees that I'm in for the long-haul and not just a quick train ride." Then he added with a chuckle, "You don't think I need to try too hard, do you? I'm real sweet tea!"

Jayda grinned and looked down at the ring, the stone sparkled enchantingly. But doubt flickered in her eyes, marring for a moment the gaze of pure joy as she wondered about the world that still existed beyond the walls of this hotel room and beyond the magic of this moment, her daughter being top priority.

"I'm not asking you to decide anything right away, Jayda. Take your time. There might still be hope for me, you think so? My second chance?"

Jayda sighed and then looked out at the bright waters of the harbor again, as though to draw inspiration. Then she looked directly at Raymond.

"Raymond, I have no plans of coming back to live in Jamaica just now."

"I know that," he replied. "Remember I asked you about property in Boca Raton the other day? On my last trip to Florida, I had been looking, you know."

Jayda sighed. She smiled at him and then took the ring out of the box. She was already wearing Trevor's ring on her left hand and she didn't want to remove it just now. Ray saw her dilemma and suggested she try it on the middle finger of her right hand.

"It fits!" she exclaimed. "How did you know my size?"

Raymond chuckled. "Your Aunt Vina had something to do with that. She gave me a very accurate guestimate. She was spot on."

Jayda couldn't stop herself from laughing. "No wonder she was so gung-ho about you and I getting back together again. She was in on this too. I wouldn't be surprised if Celia had some knowledge of this too."

Raymond shrugged and smiled but did not say a word.

"OK, Raymond. I'll wear it. And I'll think about what it means."

"I'm glad, Jayda. I want you to keep me in mind until I get to Florida." He stood up and walked past the table and took her hands. She got up from the chair and he embraced her. "I hope you'll marry me, Miss Right," he said close to her ear.

Jayda could feel her passion surging again as he picked her up and brought her back inside the hotel room.

"I believe in second chances, too, Ray," she said and kissed his cheek.

ONE OF MANY WINTERS

Monica Ronwell regretted coming to England ever since she first saw the dark rain clouds in the bleak sky, the rows of cold stone terraced houses with many smoking chimney stacks which she had thought were factories, and the drab, damp interior of the basement flat which she shared with her husband and two children.

No more mango trees, blue skies, wavering palm trees or the heat of back home. Just damp walls and cold rain-dripped windows.

The Ronwells arrived from the West Indies in the autumn of 1961—October of the previous year—and had stayed with relatives until they found a place of their own: the basement flat which was hardly fit for human habitation, the 'rat-hole', as Mr. Ronwell contemptuously named it.

Monica was sitting alone in the flat one Friday afternoon. The flat was a single room cluttered with all their worldly goods, a battered old suitcase that withstood the journey on the ship; a double bed and toddler bed crammed into the tiny space, and a small wood pantry containing the barest essentials. Food was cooked on a gas stove in the communal kitchen on the next landing up from the basement.

The rain pounded incessantly upon the chipped ledge of the tiny basement window and the concrete slabs of the pavement outside. The hardly visible fumes from the paraffin heater curled upwards towards the ceiling.

"Dear Sister Liz," Monica wrote on a clean sheet of writing paper. *"How keeping? Is it mango time out there in Jamaica now? . . . It is so cold out here in England . . . Times are hard. Very hard . . . Joe is cracking up under this hardship. He wants to go back. He has become so vicious and is always drunk. I am afraid of him because he beats me sometimes and we cannot leave each other because neither of us has anywhere to go . . . But one day I am going to return to Jamaica. I know it is hard there too, but I can cope with hardship when the sun is shining. Don't forget me, Liz . . ."*

Monica paused to think. She was not sure how to finish the letter. Some of her tears smudged the ink on the paper and nearly obliterated one of her words which she had to rewrite in a dry spot. Feeling depressed, frightened and alone, she could not remember a day that passed without a tear shed. She could almost feel her innards drying out. Soon she would be dry-eyed, hardened, callous, without a tear left, but with plenty of pain remaining.

She heard a voice outside her door, from the landing above. Someone was calling her. Too choked to reply she just sat there, staring into mid-distance, the sickly sweet smell of hair Bergamot filling her nostrils. She probably put too much in her hair along with the crooked sponge curlers. A moment later she heard footsteps on the wood staircase outside the door and finally there was a knock.

"Monica, are you in there?" It was Mrs. Croy, who lived in the flat above the Ronwells, a fat, dark woman who loved to go out to parties wearing tight crinoline dresses and stiletto healed shoes; who danced the mento and calypso, and earned money pressing people's hair with a hot comb.

"Yes, I'm here, Mrs. Croy." Monica managed to speak. She got up and opened the door which could not open too wide because one of the beds was positioned close by.

"Monica, didn't you look round the back yard?"

"No. Why?"

"Because all your clothes have fallen off the line into the mud. You'll have to wash them all over again."

"Curse the stupid clothes, man! Curse the rain, curse every damn thing! I can't stand it no more." Monica began to weep aloud.

"What's the matter, Monica?" Mrs. Croy approached her and looked at her sympathetically. "Is it your husband? I heard all the noise last night."

"It's everything. I can't stand it anymore," said Monica.

Mrs. Croy put an arm around Monica's shoulders as they moved back into the room.

"What's the use of crying though, Monica?" she said. "You will only sink deeper into depression. And what about your two children? They are young and aren't aware of many things but they are aware of depression."

"It's not only depression they're going to be aware of tonight," Monica sobbed. "There is no food in the house. Nothing. That's why I tell them never to waste any of the free dinner they get at school . . . Only God knows how much I want to leave this place."

"There is suffering all over the world, child. If you suffer one place, you can always expect to suffer at another," Mrs. Croy said kindly, her pearlized pink lipstick contrasting oddly with her dark skin tone. "Anyway, put a raincoat over your head and go out and' pick up the clothes, and I will bring down a pack of rice and some salt fish that I have upstairs."

"Thank you," said Monica, drying her eyes with her sleeve. She managed to smile at the woman who had also suffered similar hardship on first arriving in the country five years earlier in '57. She had no children and her husband had deserted her.

"One more thing, Monica," she added before leaving the tiny bedsit. "Remember that the man with the spongy red nose is coming round to collect the rent tomorrow. Remind your husband. I wouldn't like to see you and your family thrown out mercilessly into the rain."

Monica nodded wearily.

The back yard was wild and grubby with pieces of old junk piled up at the far end against the fence. As Monica bent to pick up the wettest clothes and put them into the basin she glanced up at the upstairs window of the house next door and caught sight of a wrinkled, pale old face, peeping out from behind the dull curtains. The old woman's eyes were faded, her gaze hostile. She was probably as frightened of her changed world as much as Monica was frightened of her own. The old woman turned solemnly from the window and the dull curtains fell back into place.

The factory always closed earlier on Fridays. Joe Ronwell worked there as a packer and would hang up his overalls with glee as the clock struck five-thirty and walk proudly out of the factory gates, fondling the wage-packet in his pocket.

"William's place was Joe's usual Friday night haunt where he would squander away his earnings on drink and gambling.

He arrived at William Samuel's gambling den in Lewisham at ten past six. It was a dwelling in an old grey-bricked Victorian villa with a couple of stone steps leading up to the front door. As Joe went through the gate and up the stone steps he heard music, a raunchy saxophone intoning the rhythms to which people would dance the newest dance craze, The Twist. Of course the music wasn't live. Probably just one of the many hundreds of records Williams collected to play for his friends and customers. The whole operation was illegal, the gambling, the selling of booze without a license and from a dwelling. A place where Joe ought not to be but who loved every second of his time spent there.

Joe was a tall handsome man but hardship had roughened his edges. His hands were toughened and calloused by the metals and chemicals he handled at the factory, his eyes reddened and prematurely wrinkled by booze and cigarette smoke. He knocked on William's door and a few seconds later the door opened. He was met by an outburst of joviality, laughter and greeting from William himself who ushered him into the front room where cigarette smoke hung heavily in the air and the odour of beer and gin was strong. The men sitting around the table in the middle of the room were laughing raucously as they slammed the dominoes down with ferocity. Joe was given a drink, then went to join the other men for the next game.

"Name the price for the next four games!" Joe shouted.

"Ten pounds for the man who comes up on top for each of the four games!" one man suggested.

The rest agreed and the game began.

"Pass me another drink, Will."

"Boy, you drink too fast, you know," said William, a heavy-set man with heavy eye-lids standing by the table containing booze of every variety.

"Di drink keeps up me concentration," Joe laughed. "Pass me di drink, mon!"

The game was long and Joe came out lucky when it finally ended. He wanted to play again but at a higher price—from ten to twenty pounds. This time the winnings went to another man who in turn suggested another game. The man suggested ten pounds for the game. That way he could keep the remaining ten pounds of his winning. The others protested but the man would not change his mind.

"Yuh t'ink me a fool!" he gave a belly laugh and Joe faught a secret desire to punch him in the mouth.

A woman entered the front room to take out the dirty glasses. She was William Samuel's wife. She looked weary and bothered but did not say a word, resigned.

The group of men around the table decided to start playing cards now. To them cards was to be taken more seriously than dominoes. A lot more money was at stake with cards.

The gaming continued until late into the night. Money continuously changed hands—from winner to new winner as each man won and lost. It was one-forty a.m. The hour for the final game had arrived. The winner of this game would be the over-all winner and would be the reigning champion until the following Friday when everyone would come with their unopened wage-packets.

Everyone was concentrating on this game, for the winning man would leave William's place eighty pounds richer. Even the man who'd earlier refused to part with his domino winnings joined in the finale.

Joe's eyes shifted from one face to another as the last card was played. There was silence before the winner finally gave an exultant shout.

"No!" Joe disagreed angrily. He stood up and glared at the winner who sat opposite him. "That wasn't fair. You was cheating'. I know you, Rynie. You always cheat."

"No, Joe. Rynie get the winnings fair and square," reasoned William. "You's a bad loser, Joe."

Joe, in his drunken stupor, began to curse. Angrily, he knocked his glass of beer off the table and it crashed noisily on the floor. In the tight, smoky little gambling den, there was hardly any room for dancing, let alone fighting.

William rushed towards him and grabbed Joe's arms. "None of that now, Joe."

Some of the other men got up to hold Joe back.

"Look Joe," William continued. "I warn you before about this. If you know seh you is a bad loser then don't come back to me yard to gamble. I don't want you mashing up all me things just because you lose a game . . . Come, let we tek him outside!"

The crowd of men brought Joe out into the passage, opened the front door and pushed him out onto the threshold. The door closed behind him. Joe lost his footing and stumbled painfully down the stone steps. It was raining hard and Joe was cold and wet, angry and drunk. Penniless, too. He had to walk home.

The two children were asleep in the toddler bed on the far side of the room and Monica was alone on the double bed, gazing up at the darkened ceiling. Anytime she felt a pain of anxiety at Joe's lengthy absence, she would immediately attempt to recall a pleasant memory. She remembered when she and her sisters used to bathe in the gully stream in St. Thomas, Jamaica, in the early hours of the morning and how Joe, who lived on the neighbouring land, would come and peep, unbeknownst to them, until he was finally caught. That was before she and Joe fell in love and got married . . . The wedding was at a small church in the mountains in the morning before it got too hot, while humming birds hummed as they sucked sweet nectar from hibiscus flowers . . . wedding cake, best wishes and prayers . . .

The memory finally dissolved and anxiety set in once more. The continuous rain sounded louder than ever but suddenly she heard footsteps outside the house on the concrete. Someone was descending to the basement from the street down the stone steps to the basement's street door. The key turned in the lock. The hall door opened. Then closed. Finally, the key turned in the door of the room and the light was switched on. Immediately the odour of alcohol filled the spaces of the room. Monica decided to pretend she was asleep.

She heard the door close and his footsteps drag wearily across the lino. She heard him pull out a chair from the tiny square table in the corner and sit down. She heard him begin to weep.

"Oh God," Monica whispered and lifted herself up slightly. She saw Joe sitting at the table with his head in his hands. She got up quietly and approached him cautiously but she soon realized that Joe was too weary to fight or curse.

"Joe," she whispered. "You should never go back to that place. Never go back. Bring your money home every Friday. Don't let your children starve." Monica felt a great ease, a relief in her compassion.

Joe was mumbling to himself, something about not needing that William Samuel. He could do without him and those cheats.

Monica almost could not believe what she was hearing. She wished she could see his face but he kept his face in his hands.

"Joe," Monica continued. "We can expect to be evicted tomorrow when the landlord comes and there is no rent."

Suddenly Joe looked up, his eyes so red that his pupils were indistinguishable.

"You never look in the coat pocket?" he said.

"What coat pocket, Joe?"

"You only have one coat, don't you?"

"Yes, Joe." Monica left his side and moved towards the door where her coat was hanging on a hook. She felt inside the pocket and something rustled against her hand. She withdrew a piece of paper—a ten pound note.

"Joe!" she exclaimed.

"You know how long that's been there?" he said.

"Oh, I didn't know, Joe. I didn't know."

"Since two weeks ago. Even I did forget about it till just now."

Was that how long it had been since Monica last wore that coat? Except for using it to merely cover her head as she went out into the back yard to rescue the clothes from the rain, she could not remember when last she put her hands into its pockets.

A silence followed between them.

Monica caressed the money, with a prayer in her heart and sudden courage.

"Joe, please don't go back to that place. Promise me."

"I ain't making promises to no one. No one's gonna stop me going to that place. Not even William himself. I have my differences to settle."

"But gambling differences are not important, Joe. Please."

"Don't worry. You'll get your weekly rent money to gamble with the red-nose man to keep this room. You can leave me alone to gamble for what I want to gamble."

Joe stood up. He changed out of his clothes and went wearily to bed, still smelling of perspiration and cigarette smoke and booze. Monica didn't want to sleep next to him but there was nowhere else to sleep.

"Turn off the light," he ordered. Monica did as she was told. She did not return to bed immediately. She went towards the narrow basement window and gazed out between the curtains at the eternal rain and the darkness beyond. The night's chill made her shiver and the thought of tomorrow would have made her feel ill but for the crispness of the freshly minted bill between her fingers. While Joe was still in the house she would not let go that money in case he decided to change his mind and take it back to go and gamble with it.

This winter of 1962 was her second winter in England and fearfully she foresaw more days of despair. She saw them in the crystal-ball-like rain drops on the window sill. But her fear was tempered by her husband's tears. She'd never seen him cry before, no matter how drunk or discouraged he became.

She had seen for the first time his humanity. He was vulnerable. As vulnerable as she was. She saw hope in the crystal-ball-like drops of tears on his cheeks.

OUTSIDE THE RUM SHOP
IN DUNGLE STREET

. . . West Kingston

Herbie's bare feet have never known shoes and at his age—approaching forty—the attempt to don a pair of penny loafers would probably fail. No shoe could accommodate a foot which had become, over the years, so unaccustomed and so hostile to the wearing of shoes. Taffu-ram, tackra and dutty, some of the locals would comment, laughing about him behind his back, some to his face. Herbie was known to step on broken glass and make the pieces crumble to a fine gravel, and his foot remain uncut. He was known to fracture someone's shin-bone with his strong big toe.

Herbie leaned against the wall just outside the door of the rum shop, scratching his crotch with one hand and swatting the flies out of his face with the other. His hair had long since been neglected and uncombed, growing into wild matted locks. He was not a Rastafarian. He did not believe in the things Rastafarians believed in. In fact, he believed in nothing at all. He simply liked the convenience of not having to comb his hair. And he loved to smoke the things they smoked, and use the jargon they used. The brethren would call him a "wolf in sheep's clothing".

The wall Herbie leaned against vibrated with the heavy bass-line of the music booming from Rufus's record player inside the rum shop. The booming bass suddenly dropped and gave way to treble which the tweeters on Rufus's speaker boxes handled well. The treble hissed, soared to a high pitch and then the bass-line fell in again. Herbie liked that kind of pause in the music.

"Dub—dub—dub a weh we wa'ant . . ." he chanted along with the beat, pleased at the sensation he felt. His grin showed missing front teeth and a slimy tongue. "Bw-o-o-y!" he cried in an elongated caterwaul. "Rufus a buss some chune een deh. Go deh, bwoy!"

Margie passed in the street and looked at him with an amused frown.

She was a big built woman, had thick long limbs and a thick waistline. A woollen knit orange tam covered her head; ill-shaped toes with bright red nail polish stuck out from broken sandals, bits of flabby dark brown flesh rolled out from small tears in the seam of her ill-fitting dress. But Margie laughed a lot. A hearty, husky laugh.

"Look deh! Herbie a'go shit-up himself. Watch ya!" she chortled.

"Move deh, gal, before me tear off you' hat and show yuh bumpy-bumpy head!"

"Me head not rough like fe yuh!" she said. "You nuh see how me baby head pretty?"

"I's through it was Indian man you did go wid outta Harbour Street one night. Me did know seh dat baby was never mine."

"Den i's who tell you seh de baby was ever yours? You ga'lang deh and lissen to yuh music, yah man. Me and yuh a-nuh equal!"

Margie used to be Herbie's girl, but now looking at him, she wondered what she ever saw in him. Ugly. Toothless. A real rum-head with nothing to do but to scratch his crotch and listen to dance hall music all day long. He had been different once, to look at. He used to have teeth, he used to comb his hair, he used to work. He would labor in the sun, building roads, or clearing trees. But working in the sun made him too black, she thought. It made him look too rough and dusty, reminding her of her own harsh poverty at ground-zero. But to look at him now, who could appear more rougher and more pauperized than Herbie, toothless, scratching his crotch and cadging rum from bar-flies all day? His attitude to life had not changed though: live off some lonely woman who worked and who could pay for his keep while he provided a few comforts—physical comforts—to assuage the loneliness.

Margie got smart enough to turn the tables on the situation: Herbie was correct about the Indian man in Harbour Street; the Indian man was a lonely married man who owned a little shop and needed a few physical comforts too. The affair was profitable for Margie. Not only did she get a few dollars a month from him for the baby, she also got foodstuffs and little luxuries from the shop to keep her mouth shut and not tell his wife. Margie might have bumpy-bumpy head, as Herbie said, but she was smart. She didn't need long hair for that! She grinned secretly.

Her loose sandals dragged over the dry dirt as she entered her yard a few houses down from the bar. She cast a glance back towards the bar. Yeh, Herbie looked like a wasted scarecrow leaning up there. It was a good thing her baby arrived so she could throw that thing out without risking loneliness again. That ugly barefoot thing called Herbie.

Over the yard fence came the voice of Mother May, the old woman, as she washed her clothes. Her sonorous voice rose to the tree tops, to the sky, imploring the sun, driving away the John Crow vultures. She sang,

"*He never fail me yet, He never fail me yet. Jesus Christ never fail me yet . . .*" then in the same breath she shouted,

"Cynthia! Get yuh backside outta de yard go buy de breadfruit, nuh. If I tell you again, yuh pee-pee hogwater! You hear what me tellin' you? . . . '*On Christ the solid rock I stand. All other ground is sinking sand. All other ground is sinking sand*,'" she continued singing.

"Me a go now, Gramma," Cynthia said when she emerged from the house. She was a fourteen year old whose body was still in the rawest stages of change between childhood and womanhood. Her breasts under the tight nylon fibers of her frayed old second-hand dress were tender buds filling out by the day and her plump round bottom stuck out like a duck's rear end. Even when Mother May ordered her to stand and walk straight instead of like a bitch in heat, Cynthia could not achieve that feat.

She tried to straighten up now as she left the yard. For her grandmother's sake.

"And don't chat to no pissin'tail bwoy out deh," hollered Mother May. "Me know yuh. Yuh mouth fly a hundred word a minute. Ga-lang! . . . '*Jesus is my Saviour, closer than a brother, closer than a friend . . .*"

Come twilight, Mother May would put away her day's work and take out her Bible and read, and pray for Cynthia. Cynthia growing up into a bad world. The jimmy-swing bwoy dem a'go tek weh her purity before she even know what happen to her . . . Mother May could see it. Mother May knew it. But what to do? All the girl children round here seem to follow the trend.

The sky was blue, distant and radiant. It looked too perfect to belong to them, the people in Dungle Street. The range of hills to the north looked cool, but looks could be deceiving. The strong sun was oppressive. The people around here knew what that word oppressive meant. They equated it with poverty. The radiant blue sky was like a jewel. It could not be theirs. Yet the oppressive sun was theirs because they knew oppression. They watched their sweat form salty beads in the dust underfoot. The sun's heat evaporated the moisture and left dryness once again. An oppressive cycle.

The houses tottered, some crumbled. Some had fallen. Broken fences scrawled with obscenities and names of political parties and 'Jah' and 'One

Love' and 'Local Don'. The tar covered street was cracked and uneven, the sidewalk mounds of grass where dogs did their business. Broken stones and gravel littered all surfaces—road and sidewalk alike—easy pickings for the stone throwers, hard going for the barefooted, and the people who played in the street.

Donal loved playing ball games in the street. But at the present time, he sat alone in the shade of a tree on the sidewalk. The time was still too early for ball games, and too hot. His friends would come around soon, Tommy, Luther and the rest. Then they would start to play. They all enjoyed cricket which they played noisily and with gusto, interrupted occasionally by a passing car.

Donal flashed his dreadlocks to keep away a fly buzzing near. He had strong features, thick eyebrows, strong sensual lips. Lion of Judah in human flesh. The girls loved him. He was the ladies' man in these parts. Nearly every woman was his and he belong to nearly every woman.

Cynthia passed by.

"Hey, sssssssst! Hey! Why yuh not talking to me, gal?" Donal asked. He knew Cynthia. Cynthia knew him.

"Yuh want me Gramma to kill me?" Cynthia half whispered.

"If she know wheh me know, she would do more than kill you, girl!" Donal grinned at the young woman. Over a week and a half ago on a Sunday evening when Cynthia should have been in church, Donal and she were entwined in each other's arms and in each other's bodies in Donal's small back room. He knew that Cynthia was Tommy's girl. Tommy was Donal's best friend who always played on Donal's side in the cricket game. Tommy used to boast about how well Cynthia performed sexually, particularly for someone as young and inexperienced as she. She was a virgin when Tommy met her. So spurred on by curiosity, Donal thought he'd try her. She was easy, especially as she had no mature sense of loyalty, although she said she loved Tommy very much (an emotional situation that was likely unbeknownst to her grandmother). Donal tried her that blissful Sunday and remembered everything.

"Why you lookin' so gloomy and going on like you don't want to talk to me? You don't like me no more?" Donal queried, his voice slightly intoned with mockery.

"Me like yuh, yes."

"What gives then? Feelin' guilty?"

"No. I just have sickness," she said.

"What kind of sickness?" Donal's smile vanished. She couldn't be pregnant. He did withdraw in time. He was never careless.

Cynthia stepped closer to him so she could lower her voice but before she spoke Donal voiced his thoughts.

"If yuh pregnant it ca'ant be mine."

"Me not pregnant . . ." Her voice trailed away and her young face looked anxious.

"Den what?"

"Me have sores, Donal."

"Sores?"

"Yeh."

"Wheh kinda sores?" A frown knitted Donal's brow.

"Nasty sores."

"Where?"

"Down below."

"Down below where?"

"You know where," she said self-consciously. "Me never had them before . . ."

Donal lifted his back away from the tree and stretched out his legs. He was uncomfortable.

"What yuh talkin' about?" he asked.

"Me never had them before me went wid yuh—that night," she said defensively.

"What you saying then?" He looked at her accusingly.

"Me not saying anything. Me just saying me have sores and me feeling bad-bad."

"Then go to doctor, nuh!"

"Me don't feel bad that way," she said. "Me feel bad because me went wid Tommy after that. And if these sores are what me think they are then he's going to have them too. And he's going to kill me."

Jesus God! Donal's mind exploded. *I thought I got rid of that thing. I had sores, too, but they got better. How could they still be passed on. Shit!* Donal closed his handsome eyes and thought a moment as though fearful that Cynthia would be able to see his thoughts through them. He sucked in his breath. *What if Tommy have it? God!*

Rufus spun tune after tune on his record player in the rum shop. Heavy rhythms, heavy beats. And amidst those were voices, almost completely submerged in the noise. Voices of the people in the rum shop. The doors of the rum shop were wide open to the street so anybody passing could be seen clearly by those inside. Aside from Rufus and the bartender there were two customers: Tilly and Rupert. Tilly's eyes were bloodshot and struggling to stay open, her breath reeking of rum. The appearance of her drinking companion Rupert mirrored her own. He too was drunk.

"Tilly is a duncie-head, me a-tell you," said Rupert to the barman.

"Don't lie," Tilly said fiercely. Nearly all her teeth were missing, causing her mouth to sink inwards, although she was still a relatively young forty-five-ish woman. "From me was t'ree me know my ABC backwards. You bouncing sixty and you still don't know how to spell!"

"Sure me can spell," Rupert countered. "Anybody who can spell a big thing like *cow* must can spell!"

"Can you spell *Psychological*?"

"Me never hear the word before," Rupert retorted. "See, yuh can't even say it."

"Course me ca'an. All right, who is the duncie-head now?" She challenged. "A man like you never heard that word before?"

"Yuh is still the duncie-head because you just making up words!" Rupert said.

"Ga'lang, you fool! You no know nuttin' . . . Blow de chune, Rufus, blow de chune!" she called, urging Rufus to play more records.

The bass boomed out again, this time more rhythmically than the last song. Rupert stood up as best he could and started skanking across the floor in a weak, tottering fashion. He was too drunk to raise his knee with each step of the dance.

"Mine you drop and buss you head, Rupert," Tilly said, craning her neck as she sat with her flabby elbows on the bar.

"*Dread! Jah Jah dread!*" went the songs.

"*Baddaration dah yah . . . De people demma bawl!*" "*De people are de rope in dis ya tugga-war game . . .*" "*De president a-mash-up de resident . . . Bow-bow-bow . . . !*"

Even as the sun began to make its descent after the hour of noon, the music blared on. More young men had gathered in the street to play cricket.

From the moment Donal saw Tommy he knew the young man was not completely himself. Tommy was a dark young man of medium height, hair cropped close to his scalp. Although thin and wiry in appearance Tommy's movement belied strength, the way he strode along the street in the sneakers a relative had sent him from America. He had tense shoulders. His eyes were red from smoking weed up under the house in the back of his father's yard that was rented to a man from the country.

"Ready to play?" Donal smiled congenially.

"Well," Tommy half smiled. "Me don't feel much like playing right now. I don't feel too good today."

"Anything wrong?" Donal asked.

"Well," Tommy lowered his voice. "Me know me can trust you 'cause you is me friend. So me wi' tell you; we're all men together and t'ing, so . . ." He pulled Donal away from the other boys standing around in the street. "I t'ink I catch something."

"How you mean?" Donal pretended one hundred percent innocence.

"VD."

"No! How you let that happen, man?" Donal instilled as much astonishment and sympathy into his voice as he could.

Tommy was silent for a while. Then he said,

"Me don't t'ink me coulda got it from Cynthia because she was a virgin when me first went wid her and me don't think she would go with anybody else. It could only be that nasty gal who live over on the next street: Cattie. I don't know why me went wid her."

Inwardly, Donal sighed. So it was Tommy who caught it and gave it to Cynthia . . . But no. Wait. Cynthia said she had hers after she went with me, and before she went with Tommy, Donal thought. Still, maybe it wasn't from me anyway. Must be from Tommy she got it.

After Donal managed to persuade Tommy that he had nothing to worry about, the game of cricket got under way. But it did not last long.

A loud shriek made every head turn. Even Herbie who stood at the door of the rum shop turned his head to see what was happening. Rufus was between records so he heard the noise outside. Tilly and Rupert went out into the heat and glare of the street, followed by the barman.

The shriek came again.

"You good for nothing son of a bitch, Tommy!" cried a woman. Her words continued with expletives that made the air curdle. "Uncivilized dirty dog!"

Tommy could not believe what he was seeing and hearing. It was Cattie from over the next street.

Cattie was a woman in her twenties with fleshy thighs and an even fleshier backside just about ready to burst out of her tight cotton T-shirt dress that used to be white. There was a tear down the front of the dress and her large dark breasts were partially exposed. The tiny little plaits in her hair stuck up all over her head like hundreds of antennae.

"Why yuh going on like this, Cattie? What the hell wrong wid you?" Tommy slung the bat away and stood with his arms braced at his sides.

"What is this nastiness you give me? I going to tell everybody how you have syphilis!"

There was an audible gasp from a few of the bystanders. Tommy suddenly bolted into a run, charging towards Cattie, landing his fist full in her mouth.

"Gwan, man. Gwan. Hit me as you like," she screamed. "Yuh bastard yuh! Yuh have the sickness. The world know you have it. Now you can't go wid nobody else. Now I have to go to doctor and mek him cure me before it kill me. It going to kill yuh! I hope the sickness kill you dead, Tommy!"

Tommy was too angry to realize at first that she had said *he* had given the disease to her. But the realization suddenly dawned on him as Cattie struggled to her feet, with all his friends watching and whispering. Tommy never felt so strange in all his life.

Cynthia had to wait long for the breadfruit at the Chinaman's shop. Many people waited. The Chinaman served in a slow meticulous manner, never going one ounce or one litre over the required amount and there would be occasional impatient outbursts or the more violent patrons would slap the Chinaman and take what they wanted before departing.

After purchasing the breadfruit, Cynthia started for home. On her way she decided to stop for a while at her school friend's house where she and her friend chatted on the veranda. After all, she thought, Mother May didn't start the dinner until four o'clock on Saturdays.

When Cynthia finally continued her journey home, she became curious at the gathering of people up ahead as she made her way up Dungle Street. Her curiosity heightened as she drew nearer and saw Tommy in the middle of the gathering, and a girl with blood on her lips. The closer Cynthia drew the more she gleaned from the scornful whispers of the bystanders and the more her soul became filled with terror. The sordid mess was out in the open. In a street like this, one man's business was everybody's business.

Jesus God! Tommy going to kill me, thought Cynthia. But who is that girl covered in blood? Wasn't that Cattie Arkwright?

Cynthia was suddenly taken by the impulse to run and hide. The people talked about the sickness Tommy had . . . Cynthia trembled. She thought, I want to go home and hide. But how?

How indeed. Mother May's house was a few doors down on the other side of the gathering of people. How could Cynthia possibly pass unnoticed?

Mother May could hear the raised voices in the street.

Good Lord, what a street of vice and iniquity: always a lot of shouting, always fighting, throwing stone and bottle, stabbing-up. My God! A street of iniquity.

Mother May waddled to her gate in her long heavy skirt with numerous underskirts and a pair of her dead husband's old socks. She peered down the street at the gathering. Just as she thought. Man and woman trouble.

Look Tommy down there arguing wid dat ol' pissin'tail gal. Tommy ain't a bad boy, Mother May reflected. *I knew his mother well before she died. Tommy is just a blighted boy because he mixing wid the wrong crowd. But Cynthia never chat to a boy like Tommy. She would more rather chat to the dirty bearded one wid the dreadlocks . . . I's what dem arguing about, though?*

Mother May waddled further out from her gate. Of course, she had no idea about her granddaughter's association with Tommy. In fact she had no idea about anything that went on now, except that Dungle Street was a bad street. At one time she used to know everything, keep up with the gossip, be in everybody's business, but now she had withdrawn into her Bible-sealed shell.

"Jesus Christ!"

Mother May's hand flew to her mouth when she heard the words Cattie shouted at Tommy. "Vice and iniquity, my God," Mother May whispered hoarsely in her astonishment. She gave a start as she saw Tommy punch the girl in the mouth. Mother May stood transfixed, more because of her undecided conscience rather than through shock: she wanted to run back into her yard and pretend she hadn't seen anything. She fought with the impulse to go and break up the melee. But she also wanted to see the outcome of the battle. From a distance. The latter desire prevailed and banished conscience. She saw the "dirty bearded one with the dreadlocks" reach out to restrain Tommy.

Feeling the shame in his face and behind his eyes, Tommy turned to Donal and shouted,

"Yuh see how people can weave lie 'gainst you!" he said this more for the benefit of the onlookers than for any other reason.

"Gwan, Tommy," Cattie breathed heavily. "Gwan wid you lies. I never had this thing before. I's you gave it to me . . ."

"Beat her, Tommy, beat her!" shouted a young man from the crowd. This restless crowd was spoiling for a fight. "Mash up her mouth some more. No mek no woman nasty-up yuh manhood! Fight her, Tommy."

Tommy, however, remembered what the whole situation was truly about. He had given Cattie the sickness. Not the other way round. If that was the case, then who could he have gotten it from? The only other woman he went with in the past month was Cynthia. But Cynthia had never been with a man before him. It couldn't be she. But supposing it was? Supposing she was doing a bit of two-timing and went with someone who had it?

My God! Dat gal Cynthia!

Tommy's eyes stared wide at the realization, and suddenly he found himself staring directly into the eyes of Cynthia who stood amidst the crowd. He dashed suddenly through the crowd towards the frightened girl. He clutched her arm and dragged her forward into the middle of the crowd beside Cattie. Cynthia dropped the breadfruit. The breadfruit rolled away amidst the forest of feet. A sharp-eyed woman spotted the breadfruit and stopped it in its tracks, picked it up and sneaked home with it. Roast breadfruit for dinner tonight . . .

Mother May could not believe what she saw. What did Cynthia have to do with all this? To Mother May's horror she saw Tommy draw back his fist and pound several times into Cynthia's face. Then she saw Margie step from her vantage point by a tree where she had been silently watching the incident up to this moment. Margie moved towards Tommy and Mother May could barely hear her say,

"Tommy, you cyaa'n do a young, young gal like dat, man!"

"Well, look wah she do me!" Tommy retorted.

Some strange impulse which Mother May did not guide set her feet running in the direction of the gathering.

"Lahd! Leave me granddaughter alone. Leave her. She don't do anything to you. What you want wid her?"

Cynthia had fallen to her knees, her face throbbing, confusion all around her. She supposed she was lucky he did not kill her on the spot, but maybe he should have, for all the shame she had brought upon her old grandmother who was now within range of the thickening crowd and must, by now, have learned the whole story. Cynthia's breath rasped in her throat as she scrambled to her feet. She had uttered nothing except groans and screams in between the time she was grabbed by Tommy and the violent assault. The bystanders, especially Cattie, waited and watched with wide curious eyes. They waited to hear this wretched girl's side of the story.

"Tommy," Cynthia moaned. "Me sorry, Tommy, truly sorry."

Cattie's sore lips turned down at the corners and she said,

"I's this likkle girl you get de germs from?" Cattie looked disdainfully at the schoolgirl. "I's what a likkle girl like she doing wid sickness?"

"I's who yuh get it from?" Tommy shouted at Cynthia, ignoring Cattie. "I did think you was a nice girl, Cynthia, but yuh not nice."

"I am a nice girl, Tommy. I am for true."

"I's who give it to you?" he enquired again, more fiercely.

"Donal," she said resolutely. "Donal give it to me."

"Donal?" Tommy grimaced and his body stiffened. He looked at his friend. Donal, a grown man?"

"Tell her seh she too lie, Tommy," Donal said, taking a step backwards. His words angered Cynthia and she continued forcefully.

"I's Donal give it to me. Him seh you tell him how good me do de t'ing so him want to find out fe himself. Him lead me astray, Tommy. Believe me, Tommy, do!"

"I's lie, Tommy. You goin' mek a likkle harlot like dat fool you up?" Donal's eyes flashed angrily.

"Don't call me granddaughter no harlot, you hear, mister!" said Mother May.

"She's a harlot fe true," insisted Donal. "She didn't say no to me. She have brain and mouth like everybody else!"

"You, Donal? You? Me best friend? Me have your germs?"

"Me don't have no sores," Donal defended. "They gone."

"From what I hear," Margie interrupted, "them things don't cure themselves just because the sores go."

"You went wid me gal, Donal? Wid all them girls you have out there to choose from, you take mine?"

"Don't kill-up you'self over she. She's nuttin'." Donal eyed Cynthia scornfully.

"Shot him a box, Tommy!" shouted a voice from the crowd, hungry to see a fight.

However, what there was of a fight ended before the crowd even had time to draw its collective breath. For as quick as lightening Tommy lunged forward and plunged his ratchet knife into Donal's belly. The people dashed forward when they realized Donal had been stabbed. There was utter confusion. Some of the young men grabbed Tommy to restrain him as though the deed had not already been done. Others went to tend to the wounded Donal.

"Murder! Police! Murder!" bawled Mother May at the height of her voice.

"Bring a cloth to stop the blood, somebody!"

"I's why you do dat, man?" said a young man angrily to Tommy. It was Luther, one of Donal's good ball-player friends. "You should a-fight it out. Not stab de man. Suppose him dead?"

Tommy's present thoughts remained unvoiced . . . I got shame-up bad, bad today, man, Tommy answered Luther's question in his mind. Although

Tommy had been momentarily relieved that the attention had shifted from his shame to Donal's predicament, the humiliation soon flooded back again.

"Come we tek Donal to hospital," some of the young men took him up and bore him up between them and led him away down the street followed by a number of curious people who had broken away from the main crowd. They had to walk to the General Hospital. Donal walked, his features creased with pain. The hospital was several miles away.

"You's a bad boy, Tommy, fe stab up somebody like dat," said Mother May. "But like it was Cynthia you did for, I suppose I don't mind so much."

"Me never do it for Cynthia, me do it fe meself," he said bitterly.

Cynthia, ignoring his depreciating view of her, said,

"You better run-weh and hide for a while. No mek police catch you."

"Shut up you mouth," interrupted Margie. "Nobody never call no police. I's doctor you all want now, not police. You all have to get you'self cured."

Cynthia looked at Margie. "You can tek me to a doctor, Margie?" she asked.

"Sure," Margie said. "That sickness gets worst after time goes by, you know . . . Tommy, you must go to doctor, too. And Cattie—where's Cattie? She gone already. You all have to see doctor. Donal would be a fool not to tell the people at the hospital."

Cynthia went and stood beside Tommy and said in the same demure voice with which she had apologised to him,

"Tommy, yuh seh me's not a nice girl, but how 'bout you? If me was good like yuh tell Donal, why did you go wid Cattie Arkwright?"

"Look, me is a man, and a man must be free," he said irritably.

"Maybe i's the same idea Donal have in him brain why him end up wid the sickness, too. So you was wrong to stab him up . . ."

"Dem seh most fight weh you see in de street is through man-and-woman trouble," said the barman, sweat glazing his dark forehead as he polished the bar.

"Weh 'bout hunger?" said Rupert.

"Weh 'bout de criminals dem?" Tilly said.

"Man and woman trouble is the most," the barman said. "I see so many in my lifetime."

"Dat wasn't fully a man and woman trouble," said Tilly.

"Yes it was," the barman insisted. "In a messy, roundabout kinda way, it was."

"Bwoy, what a mess," said Rupert over his glass of straight rum.

"What a rat race," added Tilly, burping softly and scratching her armpit.

"Man blame woman, woman blame man," Rupert said.

"That'll teach them," the barman smiled. "Especially that cocky Donal fella. Couldn't stand him. Me hear seh Donal leaving the neighbourhood now. None of de gal dem round here want to know him no more, like how his manhood dirty-up now. You understand weh me mean." The barman chuckled. "I hear he still takin' de medicine de doctor give him, and he got an injection 'gainst the sickness too."

"Cynthia and Tommy got medicine?" Tilly asked.

"Yeh," replied the barman.

"What a way Cynthia and Margie are good friends now. Cynthia is always with Margie baby," commented Tilly. "And Margie teachin' Cynthia how to sew, and t'ing."

"I's because Tommy not around anymore. Him gone to the country," the barman grunted as he stooped to reach under the counter for a quart bottle of white rum.

"Big 'bout yah!" Herbie announced loudly as he stepped out of the glaring brightness of the sun-dried street into the cool shade of the rum shop. In his dusty old tattered clothes he sauntered up to the bar. "Big 'bout yah!" he announced again.

"Who big 'bout yah?" Tilly twisted around on her bar stool, and when she saw Herbie she rolled her eyes to the stained ceiling and kissed her teeth.

Looking haughtily about him in his rags, Herbie said,

"What a set of people love gossip. Every time I come in here you all talking the same thing."

"Den come out, nuh," Tilly said sourly and looked away from him.

"Yuh wouldn't say dat if you knew me have some dunny," Herbie said mockingly. He reached into the tiny pocket of his tatty shirt and withdrew a wad of paper money. Everyone eyed the bundle disbelievingly.

"Weh you get dat from, Herbie?" Rupert's eyes stared.

"Me have a new girlfriend," he replied. "She kind, you see. She work in a store up side a-Victoria Park. She gimme de money fe pay down 'pon a shoes."

"Den why you no go buy de shoes?" Tilly queried, irritably.

"Me thirsty bad, you see, man. Have to get me a drink first."

"Buy me a drink nuh, friend," said Rupert.

"OK. Bartender!" called Herbie proudly. "One fi Rupert . . . One fi Tilly, too, al'doah she no like me."

"So weh 'bout you' shoes?" Tilly asked Herbie.

"Chupps, man. Plenty time fe shoes. I's a good woman me have now. Me's awright!"

HEAVENLY TWINS

My sister Hesther was beautiful when she was young. Although we were identical twins, I never thought of myself as looking anywhere as close to beautiful as she, with her long-necked grace and straight-backed poise. In our small hillside community a few miles outside Montego Bay, we were respected. We were Sister Marie Gentles' daughters. Sister Gentles was greatly respected in the local church a long time ago. Back in those days, with our white gloved elegance and dainty lady-like attire, we were the stars of the district, despite the lowly humbleness of near-poverty all around us. Through the sale of crocheted doilies to other church sisters, and the making of chutney (an art taught her by a staid English woman she used to work for as a butleress in the colonial days), my mother was able to keep herself and us in the manner to which we were accustomed, even after our father's death.

Hesther and I were so dainty, so pristine, so respectable, logic dictated that we were also untouchable. Hesther and I never married. We are now a couple of old virgins. At least, I think Hesther is too. One evening when we were both sixteen she came home late from visiting a school friend. Her dress was awry and she burned her underwear outside the back door of our hillside house. I never learned the reason why. And I wouldn't be presumptuous enough to ask at this late stage of our lives!

Now in our late sixties, the two of us live out our lives in the old house bequeathed to us upon our mother's death. Many of the people in the local district have moved away to big cities or even abroad.

One thing that disturbed me about Hesther was her sudden interest, not only in astrology but the occult. Mother raised us to believe in the Almighty God, the only true Power. She always said we were to have faith. "Faith will carry you through any storm," she said. To me, that meant if you placed your faith in other things like "star gazing" and "palm reading" then you cut your religious faith in half. Hesther does not see it that way. She believes the meaning she reads in the stars is a meaning written by God. Mother would turn in her grave! The stuff of heathens and pagans, Mother would say.

Hesther developed her interest in astrology, palm reading and tarot cards into a lucrative profession. She catered to the tourists in Montego Bay. I must admit she made more money from this than from any venture she was ever involved in but I still expressed my disagreement.

This morning we woke up to a beautiful sunrise. Insects buzzed in the hibiscus shrubs where the red petals waited to unfurl.

Hesther was in a good mood. She bathed in the outside shower and put on a billowing red dress to which she sewed decorative gold coins, giving her the look of an old gypsy. A white cotton turban covered her hair. A few years ago she would have died if any of our church sisters came by and saw her dressed like that but now that she was "rich" she didn't care. 'People can condemn all they want,' she'd say, 'but what I am doing is being validated by a worthy profit. Believe me, I am doing this for the Lord. I probably pay the highest tithes in the entire church! The deacon hasn't complained.'

Today, Hesther prepared herself for a visitor she had talked about for the past two days after she came back from a routine visit to several Montego Bay haunts where tourists found her mysticism intriguing. In one of the fancy hotels down there, Hesther met a young Black American woman whom she described as "so rich and so beautiful but so, so unhappy."

"I'm expecting her to come by this afternoon in a taxicab," Hesther said.

I went about my business of feeding the chickens and washing our bedclothes.

At two o'clock in the afternoon we heard the sound of a car. Its door slammed and the engine started up again. Where our house was situated on the leeward slope of the hill, it was unapproachable by any motor vehicle, only accessible to a donkey cart or someone on foot. So our visitor had some climbing to do, up the winding, dusty foot path to our house.

When she appeared in our yard, I was stunned. She wore a broad-rimmed straw hat and huge sunglasses that almost completely hid her face, and a simple yellow linen dress, white sandals on her feet, appearing glamorous like the women in those Black American magazines I'd seen in the store. I knew this was the woman who'd come to see Hesther. She had a hand on the crown of her hat to keep it from blowing away on the steady mountain breeze.

Looking up from my washing, I said,

"Hello, may I help you?"

"Hi, Hesther," she said, walking towards me. "How're you doing? You look very busy. Did I come too early?"

I spluttered as I tried to tell her that I was not Hesther but the young woman continued talking, "You have a beautiful home, so high up and away from the rat race . . . I know what the rat race can do to people. I know what it's done to me. Twice I've tried to commit suicide. I need to get my life straightened out. I want to hear what my future holds so I can know what decisions to make."

Suddenly, I saw an opportunity. Before telling her that I wasn't Hesther I said, "Knowing your future isn't what's going to help you make the right decisions. Having faith in your future will."

At that moment Hesther came striding out the back door in her voluminous red dress wearing a wide smile. "Hello, Erica. Good to see you."

Suddenly, Erica burst out laughing. "Twins!" she exclaimed. "Now who's who?"

"I'm Hesther!" Hesther exclaimed. "She's Josephine."

"Josephine, I thought you were Hesther, and here I am pouring out my soul to you."

"No problem," I said and watched her follow Hesther into the house.

In the beginning I could hear much laughter. Hesther was good at making people laugh and feel comfortable. However, after a while I could hear nothing. I hung the sheets on the line to dry and then went inside the house. I moved here and there, pretending to be busy, all the while listening intently. Through the closed door of the parlour I heard a curious sound, like low weeping. The poor girl was in distress.

It pained me. I knew my twin sister. She was an ordinary mortal like myself. Throughout our long lives I have never known her to be psychic or display any special powers of insight or even intellect. She was an ordinary woman just like me—only prettier—and yet there she was beyond the closed door, telling the young woman about her future. What is the future but an abstract vision in the mind that can either warm your heart or drive you insane. It must have been easy for Hesther to tell Erica about her past, even though she did not know Erica. Hesther had a brilliant imagination. But what future could she see in the palm of Erica's hand?

I heard Hesther say, " . . . You see under your little finger . . . there are no lines, neither straight nor slanted. No children . . ."

"Because of my abortion," poor Erica wept.

I gasped. This was hideous. I could not stop myself from barging into the room. It must have been the spirit of Mother pushing me in. I stood there, huffing, glaring at Hesther who looked horrified at my entrance. Erica, her large hat on the couch beside her, sat with shoulders hunched, eyes red and wet.

"Hesther, you can't do this. Not in Mother's house. What do you want to do? Rain down terrors and curses on us? The worst sin a person can commit is giving their soul to the devil. Whether you know it or not you're helping this girl do just that. Tell her about faith. Tell her about love. Show her how she can love herself so that she can face her future with a happy countenance. What you're telling her, whether it's the truth or otherwise, is not going to help her. How much you charging her? Don't tell me."

Hesther's astonished gaze turned to a furious frown but I couldn't stop myself. Must have been Mother's spirit indeed coursing through this timid body of mine.

"Erica," I said. "There's good and bad in your future, just as there's good and bad in your past. Everything depends on how you handle the good and the bad. No sensible person can expect good all the time. So Erica, you buck yourself up and keep your backbone straight. If there's a man you want, go out and get him. If you want a baby, keep trying, or adopt. If you're worried that people don't like you, say To Hell With All and Sundry!"—My hands flew to my lips. I was shocked at myself. I have never used the word "Hell" as an expletive in Mother's house before. But somehow it felt good.

Erica's lips broadened slowly into the widest smile and her eyes filled with more tears. This time tears of joy.

"You know what, you damn right, sister! You damn right!"

Hesther stood up finally, her face wearing an awful pout. "Josephine! How could you!" She stomped out of the parlour.

"And Erica," I held out my hand to the young woman and she stood up. "I want you to stay with us this evening, if you can."

"I can. I go back to the States in a couple of days."

"Good. I want you to have dinner with us and come to church with me this evening. Let no man—or woman—play God and tell you that they know your future. If they know your future then they must know their own. Only the Almighty knows your heart so only He knows your future."

"Oh yes. I'll come to church with you," Erica said, then a frown creased her brow. "Oh, dear. What about Hesther? You've offended her."

I smiled to myself. Hesther was offended because I stole her customer from her but she'd get over it. I said to Erica,

"She'll come to church. The Almighty knows her heart too."

THE VANISHING VEIL

Is it improper to yearn for innocence
Again? To yearn for a time when yearning
Itself was a splendorous pastime?
To frolic in the stream where ideas swam
And frolicked with us.
To dance barefoot in vast green fields of unconcern,
and laugh unchecked like warbling birds high
On the limbs of maternal trees.
Etch our names with fingertips in soft sands
Kissed by pure blue surf.

Is it improper to hold on so tightly to the memory
Of innocence? Innocence—that thin, delicate,
Wispy, elusive veil which once nestled protectively
Over us, like mist nestling low in a valley
At daybreak.
Then innocence, like the mist,
Vanishes . . .

And all is exposed to the hot scorching
Sun of life . . .
Until the sun sets and we return to
A memory of innocent times past
And a veil we draw close to our cheeks to keep
Us warm.

ENSLAVED BY THE BLIZZARD

Chains wrap your wrists
Bind your ankles.
Upon your brow black as ebony
Shines beads of sweat like jewels
Dripping into your eyes and
Mingling with salty tears of confusion and anger
I thought you would have escaped your slave master.
Loosed yourself from the chains and
Run like the wind into the forest;
Hidden your tracks in the swamp to throw off the
Scent of the slave master's dogs.
Instead you trip and fall in the chase.
Leave tracks for your slave master to find you
Catch up with you and
Overpower you and cause you not to know your
　　　　True self anymore.
　　　　　　　　You are just a slave.
　　　　　　　　　　　Not a man with many awe inspiring facets.
　　　　　　　　　　　　　And you have more than one slave master.
Crack . . . He's a rough-edged brigadoon, evil.
Cocaine . . . The whitest slave master you'll ever know.
And at the feast the slave master's crazy cohorts
Heroine, angel dust and all the others
With alphabet-soup names
Drink and toast to your downfall and capture
They feast well into the blurred night through to
The strung out morning
They celebrate your enslavement
While you sit with sweat on your brow, in chains in
　　　　Juvenile Hall, waiting for the judge to call your name
　　　　　　　And shuttle you from program to program
　　　　　　　　　Lock-up to lock-up.
　　　　　　　　　　　You have a tool hidden away deep inside you.

The heavy metal file that you can use to file down
Those chains, wrench those chains off your wrists,
Off your ankles,
And walk to freedom.
Toss the slave masters overboard into the deep blue sea.
Commandeer the ship of your life.
Be conqueror and ruler of your own self
Don't be afraid of yourself
Don't be blinded by the blizzard of cocaine snow.
Shine forth like the sun,
Black Son, freed from bondage
Fruitful with knowledge of your own being.
Being free.

dedicated to *"young lost men searching . . ."*

...WE DROWNED

When we were in love
We drank white wine and laughed
Till tears filled our eyes and
Blurred our smiles.
Took deep breaths as
We looked out on a clear
Crisp morning that sparkled
With a new sun and set
Ablaze the diamond universe on my finger
And filled us with the need to touch
One another in stealth in that tiny ancient
Theatre house as the play unfolded
To a velvet hush, smooth silence.
When we were in love
We swam together in a watery haze
Swam where the haze was deep
The water abundant with motion
When we were in love.
And
    there
        We both drowned.

MORTALITY

Inspiration
Expiration
Inhalation
Exhalation
A
heartbeat
No
heartbeat
We are born then
We die

In between there is life abundant
Life to do with as we please
To do with as we will or
As the Almighty wills

Life is one long wait
Like waiting at a bus stop
We can read while we wait for the bus
We can talk to those who wait with us
We can twirl our feet and exercise our ankles as we wait
Or we can fold our arms and with tight lips
Talk to no one.
Just stand there, silent.
And wait till the bus comes

But the bus will come
Mortality.
Why is there a span of life
Be it short or long?
A span of life suspended between
Birth and death like a rope bridge
Hanging high above a treacherous
Ravine
Mortality.
Abundant life
The fullness of death
After a life well spent

Mortality measures
our lives the way nothing
else does

Mortality looks back upon all
We've done and takes an account
Draws up a list.
Rich
Poor
Young
Old
Mortality equalizes us all.
The list is for those left behind
On God's green earth
Living with their own
Mortality.

THE UNCARING FARMER

He is one of life's farmers who
Cast his seeds to the wind and
Let them fall where they may
Come harvest time he
Vanishes
Never to harvest his crop
The crop wilts and dies.
Abundant pickings for the crows and the buzzards
That swoop and pluck
The ears of dead corn.
Unprotected and unurtured
The field of dead harvest becomes a wild wasteland.
The infant cried for the first time
In its tiny life
He stared into the eyes of Mother Earth and
Knew she did not want him.
The infant stopped crying and looked
Away.
I condemn you, Mother Earth.
I know you don't want me.
I condemn you.
Why did you bring me into this
Evil world if you didn't want me?
I condemn you.
I condemn all Mothers who
Abandon
       and
       Victimize their
          Children . . .
     Free of condemnation
        Free of care.

Held to no account at harvest time.
Mother wept.
She hadn't asked to be born either.
Neither had she been wanted.
An accident of time and space
A seed cast carelessly on fertile soil
In a futile place
By a careless farmer
Who roams
Free of burden

FRAGMENTS

Seaspray
    Gold Dust
        Droplets
            Pieces
        Fragments of memory
Fingers, many . . . Fingers
    Touching, linking, joining
        Dew gilded grass, much
            Heartbeat, heartbeat
      Lyrics, many
A tree, its roots are many
    Fragments of love
        Many fragments
           Much love to give
The fragments are enough for all.

A HAIKU

The willow tree bows
And kisses the last ripple
Bearing the first bud

Jagged mountain peaks
Upside down, dripping with dew
A crystal sojourn

THE HOUSE IN SEVENTH STREET

Di broken-up old wire gate
Open into di yard
An' a man name Bo a-siddown 'pon di verandah
Swiggin' Red Stripe
Him eyes swivel roun' and roun' in him head. Eyes
Red red like di sun.
Him breat' is like di howling sea in him wind pipe.
Him clothes dirty like di street
on di other side of di gate
Of di house in Seventh Street.
T'ree dogs, one name Bluka, one name Dead 'n Wake,
One name Cut-Throat
Poor Cut-Throat doan't have no teet'
Dem is shape-a dogs.
Dem ca'ant guard di house in Seventh Street.
Di two old people. Gazing away into a past so
Distant and pastel colored, di present too
Painful to bear.
Sickness, old age, di grey pair.
As old as di house in Seventh Street
Di washer woman-homehelp-cook whatever
You want to call her.
I would call her slug.
Fe her pease always bun-up and favor bed-bug.
I never see a woman who love to cuss!
When she fight
She mash bokkle 'gainst wall.
She t'ink just 'cause she big she can brawl
An' mek everybody 'fraid
In di house in Seventh Street.
Di story is not complete.
Dat woman nearly get her face mash wid a brick
By di old people son.
She push her luck too far
Playin' bad 'ooman!
I's di old people she-a ill-treat.
Di 'ooman dirty, she far from neat.

Bad t'ings happen at di house in Seventh Street.
Di rain fall, fall
In di mango tree
In di mint bush
Dere is a hush in
Di house in Seventh Street.
Bo dead on di verandah
Eyes and mout' wide open.
Di dogs stray to other parts.
Di washer-'ooman garn long time, fire at her tail.
Di son send di old people to a gova'ment home . . .
Di rain stops
        Di clouds shift.
                And dere is di sun.
Blood red.
A bullet hole
Blood smeared in elongated streaks.
As di sun sets on Di empty
Haunted ruins of
Di house in Seventh Street.

EBONÉ IDENTITÉ NOUVEAU

Eboné
Identité
Nouveau
New
Something
New
Something I knew
Deep inside
When I juxtapose the
Now with the
Then
The old with the
New
The Evil Triangle
Slave trade
Two worlds
Africa
New World
Columbus's world
We are Africans
Light years removed
Hear tell that some in Africa
Still cannot understand
The pain
Cannot grasp the meaning
The fall-out from
SLAVERY
Some never descended
The dirt road to the
Waterfront where the
Slave ship waited to take their
Brethren away across the
Vast sea to
Columbus's world.
In the new world there is
Rap music, reggae music, jazz
Music MUSIC MUSIC MUSIC
As blood is to the body

Music is to the soul
Gospel music, blues music
All the while the blood
Flows . . .
Music, culture, the umbilicus
Between Africa
And her child
The Enslaved One.
The Enslaved One
Emerges from slavery and must
Recreate himself
Eboné Identité Nouveau
A new black identity
Did the Afro start on the streets
Of Watts County, California, behind the
White sheriff's water canon
Or in the shadow of the Kilimanjaro?
Did the blues start in the Mississippi Delta
Or the delta of the Nile?
Did Rastaman vibrations start at the
Words of Marcus Garvey struggling
In Columbus's land
Or with the nomads who trudged
Ethiop's hot sands many hundreds
Of years ago?
Did Samba and Rumba and Merenge
Start in the sugar cane fields in the
Shadow of the Conquistador's nest?
Or did they start in the steamy rain forests
Of Angola?
Define
Redefine ourselves
          Coloured folks
                    Negros
                              Black
Black and Beautiful
Afro-Caribbean
African-American
Afro-Latino
Black-Hispanic

Black
    Again
        Black
            As we are
In the new African identity
There are no tribes
There must be no more tribes
NO MORE
We must no longer be
Vulnerable to
Divide and Rule
Just unity
Unity
Agree to disagree but
Unity
Love and UNITY
ONE LOVE
PEACE AND LOVE, MON
Eboné Identité Nouveau
The child with the new spirit
Returns to the breast of his mother
Then moves on
Mother sends him on his way
Renewed
Envigorated
New
Strong
But Mother, always be mindful of the
Pain of your Son, once enslaved.
Learn about his suffering
Mourn with him
Then help him to move on to a
New Black Identity
An identity of strength, Self reliance, Deep spirituality
Strengthen the umbilicus,
Don't let it atrophy
Mama Africa
Love the newborn child.

CHASTIS'MENT

I's like a judgment
Livin' by the sacrament
"Wanti-wanti, can't getti
Getti-getti, no wanti".
When we have little, we craven
When we have plenty, we no want i'.
Chastis'ment, Mama, Chastis'ment.
Me remember when we use to watch di poor children in Biafra on telly.
You used to seh "Drink up yuh corn porridge. Look at di poor children dem
    starvin' all over
Di world." An' when you garn out the room
We chuck di porridge out di window.

Chastis'ment, Mama, Chastis'ment
Whoy, Lawd, me hungry, mam!
Sorry, Mama, me never mean to t'row weh di
porridge.
Me never mean to t'row weh
di pease soup
di banana an' yam
di ochro an' salt fish
di dumplin' an' chocho
di chicken soup
di pumpkin
di rice and pease.
Chastis'ment
I's like a judgment
Reaction is on us
Yuh used to tell us, Mama, how when yuh was a child you never had nuthin'.
In the mountains you used to groan with hunger
Fetch an' carry water
Pick coffee
Go to church, sing songs
And groan with hunger.
We have everything now.
"We confuse with everything we have," you say.
But Mama, we t'row everything weh!

An I's Chastis'ment now, Mama.
Chastis'ment.
Me ca'ant tek no more.
Me wish me could find di dustbin where me t'row di pease soup
di banana an' yam
di ochro an' salt fish
di dumplin' an' chocho
di chicken soup
di pumpkin
di rice an' pease—an' di window where me t'row di corn porridge.
Chastis'ment
I's like a judgment
Livin' by di sacrement
Wanti-wanti ca'ant getti
An' getti-getti DEAD.

ON THE BEACH

Through the wavering palm fronds
The sun shoots its rays
Illuminating the white sand,
Sparking off the blue ocean
The wind sighed
Gently coaxing the fluffy
Clouds to drift away on
Their plump white bellies
Peace
Perfect peace
Joy, perfect joy.
Being at one with the world.
Gazing out at the blue yonder
I prayed with all my heart
That all the wars had ended
All the politicians sought after
The truth and became brotherly
I prayed that all the mischief-makers
And evil-doers either changed their
Evil ways or vanished from the face
Of the earth.
The palm fronds parted in
The gentle breeze
And a ray of sun light kissed my cheek
No Judas kiss
A simple kiss
God loves me.
But the blue yonder across the sea
The jade horizon
Hides the other world
The real world where
The ungodly walk the face of
The earth proclaiming their rights
Proclaiming their home-grown truths
People torn by wars, strife and strikes

Destitution, revolution, pain
Out there across the ocean
Locked behind the blue yonder.
    From here on the beach where I lay
    The palm fronds part in the soft breeze
    The sun kisses my cheek
    And I know
    God loves me.

SOMETHING BEAUTIFUL

An empty beach house
Brilliant blue sky
Blue lurex dress
Glistening in the sun
Grains of sand
Poinsettas
Exotic trees
Scent of ripened mangoes and breadfruit
Sugar cain and oranges
A gentle voice above
A softly strummed guitar merging
With the breeze
Handsome face
Asleep with the opiate of
Sea winds
Sleepy tide
Tree hooded hill side
A wind ride
Lover's side
Wheel of a gypsy wagon
The beauty of the circular Creation.

SOMETHING MYSTERIOUS

Silence.
Blood curdling scream in the night
Willo'the wisp
Lurking shadow
Footsteps in the room above
Dying candle flame
A ghostly picture in a golden frame
Falling of the fog
Thickening of the bog
Haunting cry of a dog
Face at the window
Someone midst the trees
Smell of death on the breeze
Approaching light through the storm
A bloody dagger on the hearth
Whispering voices
From mouths unseen
A child's mind
Creation
Mankind's grave.

SOMETHING PLEASANT

A deserted farm yard
Twittering birds of the early hours
The fresh smell of green
Nothing but Silence to be seen
The sharp engulfing scent of morning
The victory blue
The rays
The sun
Its going down
Red ripples in the sky
Reflections on the glassy pond
Sun subsiding to the grave
Beyond the silhouette shapes of
Spindley trees and thatched cottages
To another world
Leaving a red blaze on the sky
On our lives
On our hearts.

SOMETHING UNPLEASANT

Expression of anger
Expression of pain
Love's death
Hate's life
Uprisings and downfalls
Kings and Queens
Laborers and slaves
Revolutionaries and followers
Religion and politics
The assassin behind the curtain
Gun aimed
Bomb primed
To take a life
Precious life more delicate than gossamer
Constant struggle
Life versus Death
People versus People
Right versus Wrong
Left versus Right
Good versus Evil
Black versus white
The In-Between prevails
In that vast tundra of grey
Where young folks stumble around
With hands tied behind their backs

FRIVOLITY

Frivolity went home with someone
Last night.
Someone she'd never met
Before
Knew him
In the Biblical sense
Then he walked out of her life
And she thought it was fun.
I'm young, Frivolity said.
I have a right to have fun, she said.
Then her best friend Sara
Took a couple of sips from a bottle of soda
And passed it to her
You look hot
Take a drink, Sara says . . .
I'll pass, Frivolity says.
Then Frivolity thinks,
Sara might be my best friend but I don't know what dread disease I might catch
from the bottle if I drank after her.
But last night was fun, Frivolity thought.
I wonder what his name was?

PERFECTION

You asked the question
And I let it settle
Sink in.
But the question does
Not jive with reality.
You ask me
Why can't I be perfect?
If you want me to be perfect
Then you want me dead.
Only a dead man is perfect
He can
      Say
      And do
      NO WRONG!

LOVE IN ALL THINGS

A single piano note
A voice sings
The waves rise
The breeze brings
Love.
A child cries
Its mother croons
The heart is wise
Do not disguise
Love.
A thickly wooded hillside
A tortuous path
Laughter denying wrath
Proclaim
Love.
A single piano note
A voice sings
Love.

Made in the USA
Las Vegas, NV
16 September 2021